I'LL BE SEEING YOU . . . *DEAD*

With heavy rain beating against her window and setting the mood for mystery, Kate curled up in bed to read Rex Stout's Nero Wolfe novel *Where There's a Will*. When she finally laid the book aside, she looked forward to not having to get up early to go to work. But a few minutes after ten in the morning a delightful dream about kissing Mike in a rowboat as Sinatra serenaded them with "I'll Be Seeing You" was scuttled by her mother shaking her.

"Katie, you must get up," she said urgently. "Police Chief Detwiler is downstairs asking to speak to you."

Wide awake, Kate gasped, "Has something happened to Mike?"

"No, no. It concerns a friend of yours."

"Who?"

"Nancy Edinger."

"What about her?"

"She was found murdered out by Indian Creek . . ."

MORE MYSTERIES FROM THE
BERKLEY PUBLISHING GROUP ...

CAT CALIBAN MYSTERIES: She was married for thirty-eight years. Raised three kids. Compared to that, tracking down killers is easy ...

by D. B. Borton

ONE FOR THE MONEY	TWO POINTS FOR MURDER
THREE IS A CROWD	FOUR ELEMENTS OF MURDER
FIVE ALARM FIRE	SIX FEET UNDER

ELENA JARVIS MYSTERIES: There are some pretty bizarre crimes deep in the heart of Texas—and a pretty gutsy police detective who rounds up the unusual suspects ...

by Nancy Herndon

ACID BATH	WIDOWS' WATCH
LETHAL STATUES	HUNTING GAME
TIME BOMBS	C.O.P OUT
CASANOVA CRIMES	

FREDDIE O'NEAL, P.I., MYSTERIES: You can bet that this appealing Reno private investigator will get her man ... "A winner."　　　　　—Linda Grant

by Catherine Dain

LAY IT ON THE LINE	SING A SONG OF DEATH
WALK A CROOKED MILE	LAMENT FOR A DEAD COWBOY
BET AGAINST THE HOUSE	THE LUCK OF THE DRAW
DEAD MAN'S HAND	

BENNI HARPER MYSTERIES: Meet Benni Harper—a quilter and folk-art expert with an eye for murderous designs ...

by Earlene Fowler

FOOL'S PUZZLE	GOOSE IN THE POND
KANSAS TROUBLES	MARINER'S COMPASS
DOVE IN THE WINDOW	(in hardcover)
IRISH CHAIN	SEVEN SISTERS

HANNAH BARLOW MYSTERIES: For ex-cop and law student Hannah Barlow, justice isn't just a word in a textbook. Sometimes, it's a matter of life and death ...

by Carroll Lachnit

MURDER IN BRIEF	A BLESSED DEATH
AKIN TO DEATH	JANIE'S LAW

PEACHES DANN MYSTERIES: Peaches has never had a very good memory. But she's learned to cope with it over the years ... Fortunately, though, when it comes to murder, this absentminded amateur sleuth doesn't forgive and forget!

by Elizabeth Daniels Squire

WHO KILLED WHAT'S-HER-NAME?	REMEMBER THE ALIBI
MEMORY CAN BE MURDER	WHOSE DEATH IS IT ANYWAY?
IS THERE A DEAD MAN IN THE HOUSE?	WHERE THERE'S A WILL
FORGET ABOUT MURDER	

The *Victory Dance* **Murder**

M. T. Jefferson

BERKLEY PRIME CRIME, NEW YORK

THE VICTORY DANCE MURDER

This is a work of fiction. Names, characters, places, and incidents are either the product of the author's imagination or are used fictitiously, and any resemblance to actual persons, living or dead, business establishments, events, or locales is entirely coincidental.

A Berkley Prime Crime Book / published by arrangement with the author

PRINTING HISTORY
Berkley Prime Crime edition / January 2000

All rights reserved.
Copyright © 2000 by H. Paul Jeffers.
This book may not be reproduced in whole or in part, by mimeograph or any other means, without permission. For information address: The Berkley Publishing Group, a division of Penguin Putnam Inc., 375 Hudson Street, New York, New York 10014.

The Penguin Putnam Inc. World Wide Web site address is
http://www.penguinputnam.com

ISBN: 0-425-17310-0

Berkley Prime Crime Books are published by the Berkley Publishing Group, a division of Penguin Putnam Inc., 375 Hudson Street, New York, New York 10014. The name BERKLEY PRIME CRIME and the BERKLEY PRIME CRIME design are trademarks belonging to Penguin Putnam Inc.

PRINTED IN THE UNITED STATES OF AMERICA

10 9 8 7 6 5 4 3 2 1

For my sisters
with loving memories of Doris

"I'll be seeing you in all the old familiar places."
—*World War II popular song lyric.*

—— Part 1 ——

Friday Night Downtown

1

A HUGE ATWATER KENT console radio in the parlor, which on Monday, December 8, 1941, had carried the outraged voice of President Franklin D. Roosevelt telling an irate Congress that the previous day was "a date that will live in infamy" now offered the Glenn Miller Chesterfield show with Ray Eberle and the Modernaires singing "Don't Sit Under the Apple Tree with Anyone Else But Me." In the song a soldier was worried because he'd gotten word from a guy who'd heard from the guy next door to him that a girl he'd met just loved to pet. The description fit the girl the G.I. had left at home to a T, so now he was telling the girl in a letter not to sit under an apple tree with anyone else but him, and not to go walking down lovers lane, or give out with those lips of hers, with anyone but him, till he came marching home. No need for Mike King to fret about Kate doing that, Paulie

Fallon thought, as his mother declared, "Supper's on, come and get it."

The announcement caused her husband Thomas to lay down the *Independence*, leave his large armchair in the parlor, and proceed to the kitchen. Taking his chair at the head of the table, he said authoritatively, "There was another burglary last night."

"Oh no," said Kate. "That's the third in two months."

"This time it was Erb's sporting goods store on Bridge Street. Like the others, the break-in was early in the morning Thursday. The thieves got away with a couple of hundred dollars."

Mrs. Fallon turned away from the stove. "Old man Erb ought to have had more sense than to leave all that money in the cash register."

Kate shook her head. "What's this town coming to? And the world for that matter?"

"I think the cops should call you in, Kate," said Paulie.

"Me?" said Kate with a laugh. "Don't be silly."

"What's silly about it? You cracked the case of the missing money for your senior class trip, didn't you? And you're always figuring out the killer in the mystery books you read. I think if the cops called you in, you'd nab these burglars in no time."

"Paulie, stop teasing your sister," said Mrs. Fallon, placing plates and bowls on the table that indicated that the war had not affected her ability to serve meat loaf and mashed potatoes.

As eating began, music from the radio carried Kate back to the Stardust Ballroom in Pottstown on an evening when she and Mike King had danced to Glenn Miller's music in person. Four years ago. Back then weekly newsreel pictures of Hitler's jackbooted storm troopers in their ludicrous uniforms had looked like comic characters in a Marx Brothers movie. All she knew about Germany and Japan in 1937 came from *National Geographic* and films that had been shown in Mr. Bohannon's history class the same year she'd met and set her cap for Mike.

Her worldlier sister Jean had dismissed it as a junior-high crush which would soon pass. But they'd become high-school sweethearts, with their yearbook pictures framed by hearts skewered by Cupid's arrow and surrounded by wedding bells. Back then they had agreed that if they were to marry it would be after Mike completed college and was accepted into a law school. It was the summer of 1934 and there was, parents warned them, a depression. So Mike had gone off to college and then to law school. But barely a month after he'd earned his law degree, fate intervened when Mike was drafted into the army and sent down to South Carolina.

Now there was no way of knowing how long he would be away. The current and chilling phrase was *for the duration*. Meanwhile, with Mike away, her older brother Jack in the navy, and Jean in nurse's training, here she was, still single, still living in her parents' home, and instead of helping to win the war, working as a typist at Gordon's furniture factory.

With the meal over, Kate's younger sister Arlene assisted Mrs. Fallon in clearing the table and Mr. Fallon went into the parlor to light a Phillies cigar and settle in front of the radio for Lowell Thomas and the news at 6:45, followed by George Burns and Gracie Allen at 7:30, *Can You Top This?* at 8:30, Gabriel Heatter with news commentary at 9:00, and *Fibber McGee and Molly* at 9:30.

Seeing Paulie dawdling around, poking a mound of cherry Jell-O with a spoon to make it quake, Kate asked, "Is your homework done?"

"Don't have any. Miss Moore was out sick today. We had a substitute, and they never give homework."

True, Kate remembered, smilingly. "Care to go downtown with me?"

Paulie smiled. "Sure."

"First, I have to go to the Book Nook to see Mrs. Bee about the rally and dance."

"Are you going to buy another mystery book?"

"Possibly."

"It's a wonder you haven't read them all by now," Paulie said.

"After I see Mrs. Bee we can catch the show at the Colonial."

"I'd rather go to the Rialto. They're showing a Sherlock Holmes and a Red Ryder."

"You've already seen them."

"Yeah, but they're really good."

"If we go to a movie it will be to the Colonial."

Paulie shrugged. "What's playing?"

"It's called *Saboteur*."

Paulie grimaced. "It's not a love story, is it?"

"No, it's about a saboteur. That's someone who works for a foreign government and has orders to blow up places like defense plants."

Her brother's face lit up. "It's a movie about Nazis?"

Kate just rolled her eyes. "If you want to go with me, you have to ask Dad."

Paulie yelled, "Dad, can Kate take me to a movie?"

The voice from the parlor rumbled, "Ask your mother."

Paulie shouted into the kitchen. "Mom? Can I go to a movie with Kate?"

"Yes, but I don't want you pestering Kate to buy you useless junk at the five-and-ten."

2

"DOWNTOWN" CONSISTED OF the three blocks of Bridge Street stretching between two stores, Grant's on the east and Newberry's on the west. In the middle stood Buster's restaurant. Boasting the town's biggest jukebox, which never failed to have all the songs that made it onto the radio program *Your Hit Parade*, it was located next to Woolworth's. About a block away was one of Robinsville's more interesting structures. This redbrick Victorian edifice with a turreted corner accommodated Feicht's drugstore on the ground floor and five stories of new apartments affording spectacular views of the Schuylkill River to the east, as well as of a long gray sprawl, the backbone of the town's economy, to the west. The large steel-making plant ran parallel to an old canal, which had been supplanted by a spur of the Reading Railway. It had been founded in 1701 as an iron forge and had grown into a manufacturer of steel beams, some of which went into the Empire State Building and the Brooklyn Bridge. Just across the canal from the Robinsville Iron and Steel Company was the town's second-biggest industry, the Gordon Furniture Company.

Almost exactly in the middle of downtown stood the Book Nook, owned by Mrs. Beatrice Bradshaw. As Kate and Paulie approached the store, Kate dug into her purse, fished out a dime, and said to her brother, "You'll only be bored in a bookstore, so go into Woolworth's and buy yourself a toy. But no telling Mom about it."

Paulie drew a finger across his mouth. "These lips are zipped."

In the brightly lit display window of the bookstore Kate found *Dragon Seed* by Pearl S. Buck; *Convoy* by Quentin Reynolds; and a biography of General MacArthur, commander of U.S. forces in the Pacific, by Francis Trevelyan Miller. The new mysteries were *Hangover Square* by Patrick Hamilton; Anne Hicking's *Poison Is a Bitter Brew; Murder by R.F.D.* by Herman Peterson; Agatha Christie's latest Tommy and Tuppence Beresford, *N or M?*; and Clifford Night's rather interestingly titled *Affair of the Limping Sailor*.

Plunging into the store, she exclaimed, "I see you've gotten in a new batch of mysteries."

Tall and matronly with silver hair pulled into a bun at the back of her head, Mrs. Bee said, "I recommend *Hangover Square*. The author, Patrick Hamilton, is best known as a playwright. But this novel is a riveting fictional psychological study of the criminally insane."

"I don't know," said Kate thoughtfully. "It sounds awfully heavy."

"The new Tommy and Tuppence then?"

"You can't go wrong with an Agatha Christie," Kate said, as Mrs. Bee plucked the book from the window. "Have you heard about the burglary at Erb's?"

Mrs. Bee carried the book to the counter. "My dear, it's the only thing the Bridge Street merchants are talking about. Half of them have changed their door locks and the rest are taking the advice of the police and leaving all the lights on in their stores after they close up at night."

"Are you taking precautions?"

"I never leave money in the story overnight. Any burglars breaking into the Book Nook would be wasting their time." She paused, gray eyes twinkling. "Unless they're readers."

"How much do I owe you for the Tommy and Tuppence?"

"After all you've done to help me plan for the V-for-Victory Rally and Dance I could not possibly charge you for it."

"That's sweet and generous of you, Mrs. Bee, but all I did was work on the decorations."

"And what a splendid job you did! Your idea of featuring a poster of President Roosevelt was a stroke of genius. A Tommy and Tuppence novel is meager payment."

"Well, if there's anything else I can help out with in the preparations," said Kate as she accepted the book, "you can call me at home any night, or at Gordon's during the day. If not, I'll see you at the big event next Saturday night."

With the slender novel tucked in her purse, Kate left the store and found Paulie playing with a B-17 bomber made of lead with propellers that really turned. "Okay," she said, "now we can go the movies."

The week after the sneak attack on Pearl Harbor had plunged the country into war, the owner of the Colonial theater had settled on two ways to demonstrate his patriotism. First, he put a notice in the *Independence* that anyone in the uniform of any branch of the armed services would be admitted free for the duration of the war. Secondly, every evening's first show started with the projection onto the screen of a color picture of the flag, accompanied by a recording of Kate Smith singing "God Bless America." This was changed after two weeks to a film of patriotic scenes as a chorus sang "The Star-Spangled Banner," motivating the audience to stand and most to sing along. The evening then returned to its prewar program of a Movietone newsreel, a short subject, a cartoon, two coming attractions, and the feature movie.

As the newsreel showed ranks of soldiers in undershirts, army pants, and boots doing calisthenics, Paulie glanced sidelong at Kate, saw her go tense, and assumed she was worrying about Mike. If he weren't in the army, he would have been seated beside Kate, the two of them holding hands.

Next came a Porky Pig cartoon which got Kate smiling. This was followed by a short subject called *Crime Control*. Dressed in a police captain's uniform, Robert Benchley issued a warning that everyday objects such as handkerchiefs, shoelaces, and typewriter ribbons posed as much a threat to life and limb as criminals. Kate chuckled all the way through it.

When a preview came on for *Mrs. Miniver* Kate muttered, "Oh, I must tell Mrs. Bee about this. She'll want to see this picture, for sure!"

Paulie asked, "Why's that?"

"Mrs. Miniver is an Englishwoman, just like Mrs. Bee. In fact, Mrs. Bee gave me the book on which the movie is based."

Judging by the preview of *Mrs. Miniver*, which had a Nazi in it whose bomber had been shot down near Mrs. Miniver's house, Paulie thought it might be worth seeing. However, after seeing *Saboteur* he doubted any movie could have an ending as exciting as a Nazi spy slipping out of Robert Cummings's grasp and plunging to his death from the top of the Statue of Liberty.

Leaving the theater at nine o'clock and finding Bridge Street lively and bustling with Friday-night shoppers, Paulie declared, "I'm going to live in New York someday."

"Really?" Kate asked, as they made their way through the movie crowd to the curb. "When did you decide that?"

"Oh that was years ago. I also decided I'm going to be a newspaperman. Everyone knows that the best newspapermen are in New York. So I'll have to go to New York eventually."

Looking for a break in the street's two-way flow of auto traffic, Kate said, "Why leave home? We have a newspaper right here. The *Independence* is a very good one."

As she spoke, a voice from behind her said, "Good evening, Miss Fallon."

Turning, she was surprised to see the rotund figure of her boss. "Mr. Gordon!"

Always the old-fashioned gentleman, he touched two

fingers to the brim of a floppy gray-tweed hat. "Did you enjoy the show?"

"Very much. I always like a Robert Cummings movie."

Gordon's twinkling eyes turned down toward Paulie. "Is this young man your date?"

"This is my brother Paul."

"I'm very pleased to meet you," said Gordon, touching the brim of his hat again. "You must be the youngest of the Fallon clan."

"Yes, sir."

"You should be proud of your big sister. She's the best of my typists."

Blushing a little, Kate said, "We're going to Buster's for sundaes. Care to join us?"

"It's nice of you to ask, but I have work to do at the factory."

"Working?" blurted Paulie. "On Friday night?"

Chuckling and again touching his hat as he turned away, Gordon said, "I'll see you on Monday, Miss Fallon."

With a break in the traffic, Kate gripped Paulie's hand and stepped from the curb. "I think I'll be having just a milk shake. May I presume you'll be having your usual, a sundae with double peanut butter and marshmallow topping?"

Paulie slipped his hand from hers. "Like that announcer says on that radio quiz show, 'Give the young lady in the balcony sixty-four silver dollars.'"

"*As* the announcer says," Kate chided as they crossed Bridge street. On the opposite side, in front of Buster's was a tall, lean, and handsome Robinsville police officer leaning against a black-and-white patrol car parked at a fire hydrant. Stepping onto the sidewalk, Kate said teasingly, "Parked at a fireplug, Jim? Aren't you afraid a cop will come along and slap you with a ticket?"

Kerner smiled. "Any risk is worth taking if there's a chance the prettiest girl in Robinsville High's class of 1934 might wander by." His china blue eyes turned to Paulie. "However, I see somebody's beaten me to her."

"When did Sergeant Jim Kerner start pulling nighttime shifts?"

"Since Uncle Sam reached out his hand to tap Sergeant Jake Elwell on the shoulder a couple of months ago and say, 'Your country needs you.' With so many guys being drafted or enlisting it's been kind of hard for Chief Detwiler to find replacements so I've been stuck with filling in." He glanced again at Paulie. "What about you, pal? How'd you like to be a policeman? You can handle the Friday overnight so I can have a social life." His eyes returned to Kate. "How's Mike getting along since he traded in mufti for khaki?"

"He's doing fine."

"Next time you write to him, tell him I said hello."

"I will."

As she and Paulie entered Buster's, Paulie asked, "Who's that guy?"

"Jim Kerner. He was a year behind Mike and me in school."

"How come *he's* not in the army?"

"Jim is 4-F."

"He looks all right to me."

"He got a bad knee injury playing high-school football. That classifies him 4-F."

"Was he one of your boyfriends?"

"Why are you so nosy?"

"I take after you."

As Kate surveyed the crowded restaurant a record of "Bei Mir Bist du Schon" by the Andrews Sisters blared from the jukebox. Seeing no vacancies in the two rows of booths which formed an aisle stretching to the rear of the long, narrow restaurant, Kate looked for empty side-by-side stools among the eight at the soda fountain. At the far end of the counter sat Johnny Groover, teenage son of the milk deliveryman, whose sole purpose seemed to be to flirt with the fountain's lone waitress. Tall and pretty with her long brunette hair pulled up and held by a pert green cap, matching her uniform, Nancy Edinger appeared as crisp as a new dollar bill. At the stool near the door sat Mr. Bohannon, Robinsville High School history teacher. He had a cup of steaming black coffee before him and a bulging brown-leather briefcase resting on his thighs.

There were no vacant seats located side by side. With a sigh Kate said, "It looks like a long wait."

Turning slightly, Mr. Bohannon declared "I'll be leaving in a minute, Kate. You can have my place." His eyes shifted to Paulie. "Oh, I see you're not alone."

"This is my second brother. Since you've retired you won't have to see him in your class four years from now."

"I don't envy you, Paulie. Kate, your sisters Jean and Arlene, and Jack have set a pretty high academic standard."

"He's got what it takes," said Kate, patting Paulie's head, "once you get him interested. Tonight he learned the meaning of the word *saboteur*."

"Saboteur?" said Bohannon looking puzzled "Ah, yes. The movie that's playing at the Colonial. I hear it's quite good."

"I thought perhaps you'd seen it tonight and then decided to come to Buster's like everyone else in town, apparently."

At that moment Nancy Edinger came from behind the counter. "Hang on another minute, Kate, and I'll get you a booth. It's time I gave the bounce to the guys in number six. Those three bums, Perillo, Flynn, and Longacre have been hogging it all night long, and the only thing they've ordered is three Coca-Colas."

A moment later as the young men swaggered past, Jonas Longacre smiled lewdly at Kate, and whispered, "The three of us are goin' ridin' in my car, so how about you ditchin' the kid and comin' with us?"

"That's very nice of you to ask, Jonas," she said with mocking sweetness, "but I cannot think of anything I could do this evening that would be a bigger waste of time."

Looking as if he'd been slapped in the face, Jonas whirled round and stalked out. With eyes on the three young men as they left, Nancy said, "There's good riddance to bad rubbish."

"They want you to think they're wise guys," said Kate, following Nancy to the vacated booth. "But I can't believe they're as tough as they let on."

"There are things Freddy's told me about that trio that would make your hair stand on end."

"Speaking of Freddy, I thought for sure I'd find him hanging around in here."

Nancy's smile flickered and vanished. "We broke up last week."

"Nancy, I'm so sorry. What happened?"

"I found out he was seeing someone else on the sly. A friend of mine saw them necking in the Colonial balcony. Men! They're all alike. Nothing but tomcats! With the exception of your Mike, of course. You picked yourself a winner in him, Kate. But you know what they say, the sea is full of fish." Her eyes shifted toward the soda fountain. "What do you think of John Groover?"

"Oh come on, Nancy, you're not a cradle robber. Have patience. Freddy will come back to you sooner or later, asking for forgiveness."

"As a matter of fact he's asked to meet me for breakfast at the Vale-Rio Diner after he's off the midnight-to-eight shift at the rolling mill."

"Will you?"

"I'm thinking about it. Now, what'll you two be having?"

After they gave their orders and Nancy hurried away, Paulie gently placed his B-17 on the table. "I saw a funny sign in the window of Mr. Smith's butcher shop yesterday. You know how the government wants people to save cooking grease to help the war effort?"

"That's because it contains glycerine. It's used to make explosives."

Paulie tapped and spun the propellers of the B-17. "The sign said, 'Bring in your fat can.' Ain't that funny?"

"*Isn't* that funny," said Kate, her eyes turning toward the large window at the front of the restaurant and seeing Jim Kerner. Still leaning against his patrol car, he gave a nod of greeting to Mr. Bohannon as the teacher came out, heavy bag in hand, with an expression on his face that Kate decided was either bemused or worried. The B-17 bomber was airborne now, heading for a raid on Berlin and held aloft by two fingers as Paulie imitated the sound of engines. When more people entered, Kate said, "It's as if Buster's is the only place in the whole town open tonight." Guttural noises from Paulie's throat were bombs blasting Berlin. "Poor Nancy," said Kate as the waitress came from behind the fountain carrying a tray with their order. "I wouldn't take her job for all the gold in Fort Knox."

An hour later she sat at the dressing table in her bedroom, keeping her promise to Mike to write him every day.

She wrote:

My darling Mike,

It's been another routine (dare I say boring?) Friday. The big news is that there was another burglary. This time it was Erb's sports store. These robberies have been happening every week, and the cops don't appear to have a clue as to who's behind them.

I took Paulie to the movies. The picture was Saboteur, starring Robert Cummings. Before we went to the show I gave Paulie a dime to spend at the Woolworth store. He bought a toy B-17 bomber and has been making horrible noises pretending to fly it in combat.

I also dropped in at the Book Nook to ask Mrs. Bee if there was anything else I could do to help her get ready for the V-for-Victory event. She assured me there wasn't. She is a truly amazing lady.

After the movie Paulie and I went to Buster's. I ran into Jim Kerner, who asked how you're doing. So did Nancy Edinger. The big news about her is that she broke up with Freddy Johnson. But I'm pretty sure it's not a permanent thing. Of course, I have no experience whatsoever in that department inasmuch as you and I never came close to a break-up.

I bought a new book from Mrs. Bee which I'm going to read tonight. All is well with the Fallons. They send their love, as do I.

I wish there were something I could do to speed up the end of this war. Mrs. Bee says I've made a big contribution by helping her arrange next Saturday's rally and dance.

How I wish you could be there.
Love, always, Kate

Settled into bed with her Tommy and Tuppence novel while rain drummed against her bedroom window, Kate felt as thrilled with opening her new book as Paulie had been holding his new toy plane. Halfway through a story in which Tuppence and Tommy found themselves caught in a web of First World War espionage, she thought she had the guilty parties fingered.

When her deduction was confirmed, she turned out the light, thought about Mike, prayed he was all right, and hoped he was thinking of her at that moment while he lay on his training-camp cot. She wished there were something she could do to hasten him home.

3

NEAR DAWN SATURDAY while Kate slept in the quiet of the Fallon house on the west end, the editor in chief of the Robinsville *Independence*, Augustus "Scrappy" MacFarland listened to the sweet sound of the rumble of presses turning out the latest edition. This glorious and stirring event had been occurring Monday through Saturday for more than a century.

Seated at the center of a large semicircular desk, he was a very large man with closely cropped reddish hair. It was a physiognomy, combined with a gruff manner and gravelly voice, which most people compared to the movie character actor Wallace Beery.

Although no one during his twelve years with the paper had ever addressed him by his given name, neither had anyone cared to inquire why and how he came to be known as Scrappy. A popular theory held that the nickname was related to his fondness for scrapple. A food that was found only in Pennsylvania, it was shaped into rectangular blocks and originally had been made from leftovers of butchered pigs—hence the name. It was heavily spiced and had the consistency of sausage. Regarded with disdain by some Pennsylvanians, and contemplated with deep revulsion by outsiders strictly because of its name, it was as unique to the Keystone State as the giant pretzels slathered with mustard, the huge Italian meat and cheese sandwiches shaped like submarines and known as hoagies, and as another Pennsylvania invention, Hires root beer. Because no one had ever dared to seek confirmation, the assumption that Scrappy had been nicknamed for the food was accepted as fact. Nor had anyone, including the man who had hired him, inquired where he'd been and what work he'd done prior to his appearance in the *Independence* offices in late October 1929. For a very brief period other members of the staff saw him as someone who might have been wiped out in the stock-market crash. But that idea went out the window when he managed to bungle a story on the collapse of the Robinsville National Bank in 1930.

When he exhibited talent for covering Robinsville High School sports it was immediately assumed he had been an athlete himself, perhaps a boxer, which would account for a nose which had obviously been broken more than once. Others saw in his massive physique the possibility that he'd been a professional football player. Yet a surreptitious search of team rosters for the fledgling National Football League produced no one named Augustus MacFarland.

Except for the debacle of the bank-failure story, evidence that he knew his way around the news-gathering business appeared quickly. He also proved to be an ace crime reporter when he personally covered the first homicide in Robinsville in more than a century. Four days after Pearl Harbor, the housekeeper for seventy-two-year-old Sara Griffith had found her employer, the wealthy widow of the chief stockholder in the steel plant, lying dead on the parlor floor of her mansion. "She appears to have caught a burglar in the act," explained Jim Kerner, the first police officer to arrive on the scene. Two months later, the case remained unsolved.

With nothing so sensational as a murder for the current edition of the newspaper, Scrappy had divided the front page between a pair of stories: the abrupt and unexplained resignation of junior-high-school principal William Street and the break-in at Keinard's dry goods store early Thursday morning, featuring an interview with Sergeant Kerner, who had speculated to reporter Dick Levitan that the thefts were the work of a gang.

Page one also included a story about the Robinsville High School Phantoms football captain, Johnny Groover. The son of a well-liked milkman had been offered a four-year athletic scholarship to Notre Dame. Completing the layout was a box reminding readers planning to attend the V-for-Victory Rally and Dance that they would be expected to contribute either cash or canned food to one of several war-relief charities.

At six o'clock as Scrappy listened to the presses below, feeling pleased with the edition and looking forward to a breakfast of scrapple and eggs at the Vale-Rio Diner, the phone on his desk rang. His answer was polite but impatient, "Good morning, *Independence* city room."

The caller did not have to identify himself. There was no mistaking the high-pitched, reedy voice of undertaker Ed Polanksy. "Scrappy, get out to Indian Creek Road a mile past the gate to the army hospital construction site. There's a dead body in a ditch out there and from what Tom Detwiler told me on the phone just a minute ago it looks like Robinsville's got itself another murder. A couple of kids on their way to do some ice-skating on the creek found her."

Scrappy lurched to his feet. "The victim's a woman?"

"It appears to be a girl by the name of Nancy Edinger."

"Now what in blazes could she have been doing way out there?"

"It is a lovers lane, Scrappy."

"Thanks for the tip, Ed. I'll see you at the scene."

4

As Scrappy's car made the turn from Route 29 onto Indian Creek Road one word, one act, dominated his mind. Murder! The willful and unlawful taking of a life. So much a part of the human condition that the first one showed up after only three chapters of the Holy Bible. God had said to Cain, "What hast thou done? The voice of thy Brother's blood crieth to me from the ground." Since then, the earth had soaked up a whole lot more.

Now, murder was the coin of the realm. Every newspaper's bread and butter. And how much more compelling a story when the victim was a young girl, Scrappy thought, as the car bumped slowly through a dark tunnel of overarching leafless tree limbs. The narrow road that was hardly more than two parallel paths laid out years ago by cattle. Now it was famous as a lovers lane. After traveling half a mile Scrappy parked behind Ed Polansky's black Cadillac hearse, its rear door standing open.

Ahead in a flood of lamplight stood a cluster of men. Rain, which had come down heavily until well after midnight, was now an annoying drizzle. It meant a muddy mess for Tom Detwiler, Jim Kerner, a couple of other cops, and Ed Polansky to tramp around in. Pausing to light a cigar, Scrappy wished he'd thought to wear galoshes.

With a glare of displeasure as Scrappy approached, Chief Detwiler growled, "Get the hell outta here, MacFarland. How did you find out about this already?"

Careful not to give away a source, Scrappy quelled a reflex to glance at Polansky. "Let's just say I got a tip."

"If I find out it came from one of my men," Detwiler grumbled, "I will have the son of a bitch's badge, and then I'll take off his hide."

"You have my word it wasn't one of yours, Tom," Scrappy said. "But I'm here, so what can you tell me?" His searching eyes shifted to the body draped with a shiny, black rubber sheet. "Do you know how she was killed?"

"Who told you it's a she?"

"I'm not revealing my source, Tom. I'm sure Ed has already told you how she was killed, and it's going to be in his report, so let's skip the formalities, okay?"

With a nod from Detwiler, Polansky answered, "She was manually strangled."

"Was it a sex thing?"

"There's no indication of it. Of course, I'll be looking for that when I do the autopsy."

"Time of death?"

"The ground under the body is soaked," Polansky explained, "so she was left here after twelve o'clock. The kids found her around seven."

Wearing a yellow rain slicker, Jim Kerner stepped forward. "It has to have happened after eleven o'clock."

Scrappy asked, "Why do you say that?"

"She was working at Buster's restaurant last night. The place closes at eleven on Friday."

"You personally saw her there?"

"Only through the window. She was having a long conversation with a customer by the name of Kate Fallon."

"I know her," said Scrappy. "She might be helpful to you, Chief."

Detwiler shrugged. "Why so?"

"I've found her to be quite intelligent and a very observant young woman."

"Okay," said Detwiler, "that's a start. I'll talk to her after I break the bad news to the dead girl's mother."

"Excuse me, boss," said Kerner, "but I think the person we ought to be talking to is the girl's boyfriend."

"And who, pray tell, might that be?"

"His name is Freddy Johnson. The word around town is that she'd dumped him."

"Okay. While I see the mother and the Fallon girl, you go have a chat with Freddy."

5

WHEN KATE FALLON opened the front door and saw the dark blue uniform with embroidered gold eagles in shoulder epaulets, and a cap with gold laurel wreaths on the brim, she gasped in astonishment. Although big-bellied and ruddy-faced enough to play Santa Claus at the American Legion post's annual Christmas party for needy children, the chief of police greeted her with a grim look. "I'm terribly sorry to bother you on a Saturday morning, Miss Fallon, but I do have to talk to you."

"Of course, sir. Come into the parlor."

Doffing the cap, he blurted, "I'm afraid I have bad news, Miss Fallon. Nancy Edinger was found dead this morning."

Kate sank into her father's favorite chair. "It can't be. Nancy's only nineteen years old! She was never sick. She never missed a day of school."

Detwiler nervously turned the cap between thick fingers. "I'm afraid it gets worse, miss. Nancy Edinger was murdered last night."

"That's impossible. Who would want to murder Nancy?"

"I'm hoping you can be of help on that score."

Kate shook her head. "I don't see how."

"I understand you talked with her last night at Buster's restaurant."

"That's right. She waited on my brother and me. We went to Buster's after the first show at the Colonial."

"What time did you leave Buster's?"

"Around ten o'clock."

"How did Nancy seem to you?"

"She seemed perfectly normal."

"Sergeant Kerner says he saw you and Nancy having quite a long conversation," Detwiler said.

"We talked, but I wouldn't call it a long conversation."

"What was it you talked about?"

"I suppose you could say it was girl talk."

Detwiler paced the small room. "I'd appreciate it if you could be more precise."

"We chatted a little about her breaking up with her boyfriend."

Detwiler stopped and drew a small notebook from a pocket. "That's Freddy Johnson?"

"Yes."

"Did Nancy tell you why they broke up?"

"She found out he'd been seeing someone else."

"Who was he seeing?"

"I have no idea."

"Was Nancy upset about the break-up?"

"She seemed to be taking it well. She asked me what I thought of another boy who was in Buster's last night," Kate told him.

"What's his name?"

"John Groover."

"The high-school football star?"

"Yes. I told Nancy I thought she could do better."

"That was the entire conversation?"

"Yes."

"How would you describe her overall demeanor last night?"

"Rushed. Buster's was awfully busy. If it hadn't been, she might have talked to me then, instead of asking if she could come to see me tomorrow. Meaning today. When the doorbell rang I thought it was her."

Detwiler slid the book into a pocket and smiled. "Scrappy MacFarland tells me you're a very observant person. Did you notice anyone in Buster's last night who, in retrospect, you think might have been exhibiting any special interest in Nancy?"

"Only that Johnny Groover was flirting with her."

"Other than him."

"There was one incident, which was nothing, really. When Paulie and I came in there was no booth available for us. Nancy complained about three guys who'd been occupying one of the booths all night and having only Coca-Colas. She ordered them to leave."

"Did they?"

"Yes."

"Do you know who they were?"

"Tony Perillo, Tommy Flynn, and Jonas Longacre."

Detwiler grunted. "That's quite a lovely trio. They left without a fuss?"

"Jonas made a remark to me on his way out, but it had nothing to do with Nancy."

"Were they hanging around in front of Buster's when you and your brother left?"

"If so, I didn't see them. Jim Kerner might know. He was in front when Paulie and I went in and he was still there when we left."

"Can you tell me who else was in Buster's?"

"Mr. Bohannon was there."

"The teacher?"

Kate nodded.

"Anyone else you can recall?"

"The rest were moms and dads and kids."

Detwiler flashed his Santa Clause smile. "Thank you very much, Miss Fallon. You've been helpful. Again, I apologize for disturbing your Saturday."

"I don't see how I've been at all helpful. Last night was a typical Buster's Friday night."

"I'm deeply sorry about what happened to your friend Nancy," said Detwiler as he went to the door.

"Do you have any idea who did it?"

"It's much too soon for that, miss. But rest assured we'll find him."

"I'm sure you will, Chief Detwiler, and I know this is none my business, but if you think Freddy Johnson could be the one, you're wrong. I knew them both. Freddy was truly and deeply in love with her. And she with him. Freddy hoped to make up with her."

"How do you know that?"

"Nancy told me Freddy had asked to meet her Saturday

morning—this morning—at the Vale-Rio Diner for breakfast."

"Did Nancy say if she was going to meet him?"

"She said she had to think about it."

Detwiler donned his hat. "Thank you again, Miss Fallon."

Closing the door, Kate slowly shook her head, and muttered, "No, no, it just won't do."

6

FOR THE SECOND time in a little over two months Scrappy MacFarland ordered the presses in the basement stopped and the front page of the *Independence* remade. He'd done so the evening of Sunday, December 7, with news of the Japanese attack on Pearl Harbor. Now as the presses waited in silence, the city room above was alive with the clatter of a pair of typewriters as Dick Levitan and he batted out what little they knew on the life and violent death of Nancy Edinger.

From a few clippings in the files Levitan pieced together the girl's history—a notice of the birth of a daughter to Mary and Joe Edinger, a foreman in the rolling mill, now deceased; a photo of little Nancy in a Gay Street Elementary School Pageant; a picture of her along with six other pretty girls in white skirts and sweaters with pom-poms in their hands; and a mention that she had been named to the National Honor Society. A recent picture, taken for Nancy's yearbook in which she had been voted by her classmates as the girl with the sunniest smile, had been borrowed from the grieving mother. Mrs. Edinger had also informed Levitan that tentative plans had been made for the funeral. The viewing would be held on Tuesday evening at Edward J. Polansky's funeral home, a mass at St. Sophia's Church on Wednesday at eleven in the morning, and burial in Gates of Heaven cemetery.

A news story consists of five w's—who, what, where, when, why—and an h for how. The where, when, and how the promising life of Nancy Edinger had been extinguished would appear on the front page with a rare byline. There had not been a story in the *Independence* which had been written by Augustus X. MacFarland since the murder of Sara Griffith. But the discovery of that still-unsolved atrocity had been made at a time of day which had not required stopping the presses and remaking page one. As to why Nancy had been killed, *Independence* readers would have to wait for the police to make an arrest and obtain a confession. Nor could his story provide them with the name of a likely suspect.

With the stories written and handed to two typesetters in the basement, Scrappy lit his first cigar since the one at the murder scene, took two puffs, watched Levitan put on a coat that exaggerated his small frame and a navy blue knitted hat both to protect and conceal the baldness of which he was always painfully conscious, and asked, "So, Richard, who do you think did it?"

"Who else? The ex-boyfriend."

Scrappy removed the cigar and examined the burning end. "Why?"

"Only he can tell us that. And maybe he doesn't know himself. It was probably what the French call a *crime passionel*. It happened on a lovers lane. He wanted to, uh, kiss and make up. She didn't."

"Polanksy says there was no sign this was sexual."

Levitan pulled the cap tighter and lower. "You know what I like about you, boss?"

The cigar went back into Scrappy's mouth. "I'm not sure I want to know."

"Even though you're a hell of a good editor," said Levitan, pulling up the collar of the oversize coat, "deep down inside you're still working the crime beat."

Scrappy smiled proudly. "You know what I think I ought to do right now? A follow-up for the Monday edition."

"You'll have your follow-up when the cops arrest the ex-boyfriend."

"You figure this murder is that open-and-shut?"

"Here's what'll happen, if it hasn't already. Our intrepid chief of police will tap his meaty mitt on the shoulder of this kid Freddy Johnson, causing the kid to wet his pants and blurt out a detailed confession."

"What if he doesn't? What's the lead story on Monday? What's our follow-up?" Scrappy asked.

"We run the headline from the Sara Griffith murder two months ago. 'Police Baffled.' "

"That's what troubles me. I'm afraid Detwiler is still so embarrassed about not solving that one that he'll rush to judgment on this one."

Levitan headed for the door. "Are you telling me you think the Johnson kid didn't do it?"

"I'm just thinking ahead to Monday and a follow-up story."

Levitan grunted. "You're acting like an old fire horse who catches a whiff of smoke."

He was right, of course, Scrappy thought, as Levitan left him alone in the city room. There was nothing sorrier than some old fart of a newspaper editor who missed being in the harness of a crime reporter. Satisfied that the Saturday edition was on its way to subscribers, albeit a couple of hours late, he stepped from the newspaper office into a chilly morning with a clearing sky. At the moment only a handful of people knew of the murder of a girl with a sunny smile. Probably, few had ever heard of Nancy Edinger. But in a little while she would be the talk of the town. Tonight along Bridge Street as folks went out to dinner, shopped in the stores, and watched the movie at the Colonial each would know all about Nancy's murder—all except who had tightened hands around her slender neck to choke the life out of her.

Yet Scrappy understood as he got into his car to drive to the Vale-Rio Diner for a later-than-usual breakfast of scrapple, eggs, and crisp bacon that by now there was a growing number of Robinsville's residents who would not learn of the death of Nancy Edinger in his paper. They already knew of it. They'd learned as soon as Chief Detwiler's car had pulled up in front of Mrs. Mary Edinger's house with something to say that was every mother's dread, and which a great many mothers all over the country with sons in uniforms would have to hear sooner or later—that she had outlived her child.

• • •

In a small town, learning of anyone's death rarely had to wait for an announcement in the local newspaper. Some would have observed the departure of Polansky's hearse. Certainly, the boys who'd discovered Nancy's body would have told of their adventure. Those to whom they'd related their find would have gotten on the telephone or rushed to inform next-door neighbors. Others would have seen Tom Detwiler's small fleet of speeding police cars, their rooftop lights flashing, and then made calls in hopes of finding out what had happened. That there had been a murder would spread faster than the radio gossip from the mouths of Louella Parsons, Hedda Hopper, and Jimmy Fiddler. Faster even than a breathless Walter Winchell on his Sunday broadcasts, punctuated with urgent-sounding dots-and-dashes tapped out on a fake telegraph key by Winchell himself, as he alerted "Mr. and Mrs. North America and all the ships at sea" to the news as only he saw it. Of course, there was nothing in the killing of a teenage girl that would interest an entire nation. But in a small town murder made ripples like a stone thrown into a pond.

Consequently, when Kate Fallon phoned Beatrice Bradshaw to report the shocking news, the proprietor of the Book Nook had already learned of it after seeing Chief Detwiler arrive at the house next door to break the news to Mary Edinger. What surprised Mrs. Bradshaw was learning that Chief Detwiler had interviewed Kate.

Sounding uncharacteristically distraught, Kate angrily asserted, "That foolish man seems to have made up his mind that Nancy was murdered by her boyfriend,

Freddy Johnson. Mrs. Bee, I've known Freddy all his life. He is not capable of murdering anybody, least of all Nancy."

"My dear, I've known Tom Detwiler a long time. I have never known him to act rashly. I'm sure he had a sound reason to come see you."

"He said it was because I was one of the last people to speak to Nancy on Friday night. He really wanted to know if it was true that Nancy had stopped dating Freddy. Now, I ask you, Mrs. Bee, is breaking up a reason to kill someone?"

"History and literature are overflowing with such instances. If the young man is innocent, he'll be able to prove it."

"In this country, Mrs. Bee, a man is not required to prove his innocence. The authorities have the burden of proving guilt beyond a reasonable doubt."

"I'm aware of that precept, my dear. It was invented in my country."

"Of course it was. I am sorry, Mrs. Bee. I'm just furious that Freddy may be the prime suspect in a murder I know he couldn't have committed."

"I understand completely how you feel, Kate, but there is nothing you or I can do about it, is there? I appreciate that Nancy and this boy were your friends, but beyond that, I can't see why it should be any of your concern."

With a long sigh, Kate said, "You're probably right, Mrs. Bee. You usually are. This is a terrible thing to happen just a week before the V-for-Victory Rally and Dance. Maybe we ought to think about canceling it. Or at least announce a postponement."

"I had the same thought, so I spoke to Mary Edinger about it. Her exact words were, 'A lot of people have been looking forward to it. Nancy certainly was. It will give people a way to contribute something to the war effort. The rally and dance, like life, must go on.'"

— Part 2 —

V for Victory

7

ONLY ONE WEEK before the Edinger murder, there had been a different argument over holding the dance. It had been one of tradition versus the propriety of engaging in gaiety during wartime.

The argument in favor had been espoused by town councilman, music store proprietor, funeral director, and coroner Edward J. Polansky. To celebrate Robinsville's incorporation in February 1848, he pointed out, the town council had decreed a celebration. So successful was this Winter Carnival that it became not only an annual tradition, but a cherished one, along with the annual Dogwood Festival and parade each May. The impassioned speech had been rich in local lore and a fervent plea for a bold display of the town's determination not to let concerns about current events overshadow the past.

The propriety argument, contended by Councilman

Herbert Smith, was that the Winter Carnival had been suspended for two years of the Great War of 1917–18. At that time the council had deemed it wrong to hold a party when "our boys" were "over there" fighting "the war to end all wars."

This position provided precedent for those who had opposed having the dance, in Mr. Smith's equally impassioned words, "so soon after the tragedy of Pearl Harbor."

What happened next was hailed by the editor in chief of the Robinsville *Independence* in a front-page editorial:

> *Appreciating both viewpoints, Mrs. Beatrice Bradshaw proposed a brilliant, deadlock-breaking compromise by which the annual event would be presented as a charitable function of the Robinsville Women's League, with the name of the occasion being changed to the "V-for-Victory Rally and Dance." Those attending will be asked to bring suitable items, such as clothing and canned foods, which will be contributed by the ladies to Bundles for Britain and various other war-relief agencies. A booth will also be set up by the Farmers' National Bank for sale of Victory Bonds.*
>
> *In recognition of Mrs. Bradshaw's leadership in other charitable undertakings the town council voted unanimously to appoint her chairwoman of the occasion. In that capacity she announced her first decision. As· was the custom for past Winter Carnivals, the event will be held in the gymnasium of Memorial Junior High School.*
>
> *A second decision, however, ran into difficulty. When Mrs. Bradshaw proposed that decorations in*

the gym include a display of photographs of the heads of state of the Allies an objection was raised concerning exhibition of the Soviet Union's Josef Stalin, whom Mayor John Cantrell denounced as "just as rotten a dictator as Hitler."

This difficulty was also handled by Mrs. Bradshaw. She proposed that flags of all Allies be displayed, but the portrait of only one leader: President Roosevelt.

Given Mrs. Bradshaw's proven ability as a diplomat, it is the opinion of this newspaper that FDR immediately find a significant post for this very able lady in the war effort, perhaps in her native London, where, we are confident, she will prove as formidable in handling Winston Churchill as she has been in dealing with our Town Council.

On second thought, we would do well to keep her our secret weapon right here in Robinsville.

Looking forward to the rally and dance, Scrappy had made up his mind to dance at least once with Beatrice and have a turn around the floor with a pretty young woman who had recently walked into the *Independence* city room looking for help.

In a burst of enthusiastic support of her friend's role as chairman of the organizing committee, Kate Fallon had offered her own services in arranging for decorations. Obtaining flags of the five allied nations had been rather easy. The manager of George Washington Fabric Company of Valley Forge agreed to provide them at no cost.

Considering the problem of finding a suitable portrait of President Roosevelt, Kate had judged those which hung on walls of nearly every house, office, and factory in Robinsville to be too small for the occasion.

"Putting up one of those puny little things, or even a lot of them," she said in taking the matter to Mrs. Bee, "would be an insult to FDR. What we need is a *huge* picture of him."

After mulling the dilemma a moment, Mrs. Bee said, "I think the person you should talk to is Mr. MacFarland at the newspaper. He's always seemed to me to be quite a resourceful chap. However, I have heard he's a dyed-in-the-wool Republican."

Mindful of the warning, Kate strode purposefully from the Book Nook and two blocks to the newspaper, then inside and up to the semicircular desk. With arms folded, she looked down at the burly man at its center and blurted, "I have something to ask of you, Mr. MacFarland."

Smoking the stub of a cigar, wearing a green eyeshade, his thick, hairy arms sticking from rolled-up sleeves of a white shirt without a necktie and a large right hand gripping a blue pencil, he did not look up at her. "If it's a job you are looking for, miss, we are not hiring secretaries."

"I happen to have a very good job, thank you. But if I did want to work for your newspaper it would be as a reporter."

"Be brief. I have a paper to get out."

"Very well, but first I must remind you that there is a war on and in my opinion it is the duty of every person to set aside one's political affiliation for as long as we are in it."

"I agree a hundred percent. So, what's your point?"

"The point is, I need a picture of President Roosevelt—a very . . . big . . . one. I was hoping that you could be of help to me in finding one, in spite of you being a Republican."

Jerking the cigar from his mouth, he glowered. "Darling, I don't know where you got that idea, but for your information, I have voted straight Democratic since James M. Cox ran for president in 1920 with Franklin Roosevelt as his running mate. What do you want this big picture of FDR for?"

"It's going to be the centerpiece of the decorations for the V-for-Victory Rally and Dance. I intend to hang it in the center of a display of the flags of the Allies."

"How can you possibly do that?"

"What do you mean?"

"You'll have five flags."

Frowning, she said, "I guess I didn't think it through."

"May I make a suggestion?"

"Of course."

"What about putting FDR between *two* U.S. flags?"

"That's it! But I need the picture of FDR. I've been led to believe you could advise me where I can get one."

"You leave it to me, Miss, uh, what's your name?"

"Catherine Fallon. Everyone calls me Kate."

"Well, Kate, if I can't drum up a really big FDR mug shot from the local Democratic committee, I'll have to put in a call to the national committee. And if that doesn't pan out, I'll just have to go straight to a friend of mine in the White House."

With a little laugh she said, "You're joking."

He returned the cigar to his mouth. "One thing I learned a long time ago is never to joke with a woman who's got her mind set on something, whether it's the wrong outcome of a murder trial or a presidential portrait. What makes you suppose you could cut the mustard as a reporter?"

"I'm curious about things. I'm good at getting to the bottom of things. I keep up with the news. I'm told I also write well."

"Who told you that?"

"My teachers."

"Ah, I see! Little essays about what you did last summer?"

"I also wrote for the school newspaper, *Purple and White*."

"What did you write about?"

"School events, of course."

"The best reporters get their start covering sports."

"Only boys got to handle sports for the *P and W*."

"Naturally."

"It's only natural because the people who hire people who cover sports are men."

"The reason females don't get to cover sports, in one word, is locker rooms."

"That's two words."

"Come on, you know what I mean. Girls and women don't belong in boys' and men's locker rooms."

"Not so long ago people said girls and women had no business being riveters, or serving in the army or navy."

"That's only because there's a war on."

"And when the war's over you'll expect them to go back to what they did before."

Scrappy chewed the cigar. "I'll tell you what I think, miss. I think you've been talking about the role of women with Beatrice Bradshaw."

"Mrs. Bee is a very intelligent woman."

"You'll get no argument on that from me after the nifty way she had the Town Council wrapped around her finger over this V-for-Victory event. I can hardly wait to see how it all turns out. Tell Beatrice I'll give her a call when I have the FDR poster in hand."

"Will you be attending the event?"

"I wouldn't dream of missing it. But since I'm doing you a big favor in getting you the FDR poster, I'll expect something in return, namely a dance with you."

8

OCCUPYING AN ENTIRE block of Second Avenue, Memorial Junior High School had been built in the 1920s to honor Robinsville men who had been killed in what was now being called the *First* World War. By virtue of its large auditorium and an enormous gymnasium, the school became the venue not only for scholastic and intra- and intermural indoor athletic contests, but the place for events of the larger community. These included performances of touring entertainers ranging from magicians to orchestras and even grand-opera stars. And since completion of construction, the gymnasium was the site of the Winter Carnival, with its fanciful decorations celebrating both the season and the founding of the town.

As Kate entered the gym with Beatrice Bradshaw on Saturday afternoon, four hours before the doors would be open for the V-for-Victory Rally and Dance, the colors she found were not snowy white and icicle-silver, but red, white, and blue. Flanked by two American flags with the banners of Britain and France on the left and China and Soviet Union to the right, stood an eight-foot, black-and-white poster of President Roosevelt with a long black cigarette holder jutting rakishly from his toothy grin, his little Scottish terrier in his lap.

Looking at the giant portrait, Kate turned to Beatrice with a worried expression. "Gosh, I hope people won't think this has become a Democratic party rally."

"My dear, I believe you will find that for all but the most rabid Republicans, the fact that Mr. Roosevelt is a Democrat became irrelevant when the first Jap bomb exploded at Pearl Harbor. Even the America First crowd and their leading spokesman, Charles Lindbergh, have come to recognize that the United States getting into the war was not only inevitable, but necessary. I think you have done a splendid decorating job. My congratulations."

When Scrappy MacFarland entered the gymnasium a few minutes after seven o'clock the Robinsville High School Swing Band was into its third number and a trio of girls was presenting a passable version of the Andrews Sisters with "Boogie Woogie Bugle Boy." By the time he had helped himself to a small cup of a fruity punch that would have been marginally okay if it had been spiked with a fifth of bourbon, the tune blaring from the bandstand was "Jersey Bounce."

He made his way around the edge of a dance floor crowded with a mass of flailing arms and twisting torsos performing a dance aptly named the jitterbug. Along the way he nodded greetings to the onlooking members of the older generation, who in their time had made similar public spectacles of themselves doing the Lindy Hop, the Black Bottom, and the Charleston.

Halcyon days back then! The war to end all wars had ended, Wall Street was bullish, the whole country was flush, and you couldn't find anyone who really disagreed with President Coolidge's confident declaration that the business of America was business. Then it all went bust in 1929 to the theme song "Brother, Can You Spare a Dime?"

It seemed that nobody knew what to do to fix things before Franklin D. Roosevelt put his hand on a Bible in March 1933. Yet even he had a devil of a time saving capitalism, until Japanese bombers rained destruction on a place in Hawaii which few people in the United States had heard about before December 7, 1941.

Now, here was an enormous flags-flanked photo of a third-term FDR grinning while a mass of young Americans danced their hearts out. Not knowing what the future held for them, they had embraced the timeless notion that the best thing to do in time of war was eat, drink, and be merry, even if the libation at hand was spineless.

Spying Kate Fallon standing alone to the side of the bandstand, Scrappy thought she looked like Scarlett O'Hara at the big dance in *Gone With the Wind*, but without a Rhett Butler to whirl her onto the dance floor. Sidling next to her, he said, "What do you say you and I show these silly kids the proper way to, what's the current expression, cut a rug? That is if this band ever gets around to playing something slow."

"It's my understanding," she replied, "that for a contribution to the Red Cross of no less than five dollars the band will accept a request. When they were rehearsing this afternoon they did a very nice rendition of 'Stardust.'"

"Stay where you are," Scrappy said, digging a hand into his back pocket for his wallet, "then you and I will treat this crowd to dancing the way it should be done."

While he elbowed his way toward the bandstand like a lumbering yet graceful whale plowing through an undulating school of sardines, Kate observed another figure as tall and stately as a clipper ship cutting a swath through the swirling sea of dancers. Reaching her, John Bohannon declared, "Beatrice informed me that congratulations for the decorations belong to you. The Roosevelt portrait and the Allied flags were a stroke of genius."

"That's very kind of you," said Kate, peering across the gym and noticing that Freddy Johnson had arrived in the company of a girl she did not know. "As to flags," she continued, "I can't claim any of the credit. They were Mr. MacFarland's idea."

"He's quite a fellow. He's been of tremendous help to me in carrying out my research."

"Oh? Research into what?"

"I'm writing a book. That's what I was doing the night you saw me in Buster's. I'd spent the evening rummaging through files in the archives of the *Independence*."

"Is it a history?"

"It's a novel based on a murder mystery."

At that moment Scrappy returned. "I hope you've got your dancing pumps on, Kate," he exclaimed. Turning to Bohannon, "John, if you're looking for a dance with this charming young lady, you'll have to wait. I've got her for as long as the fifty bucks I just slipped the bandleader to play every slow number in the group's repertoire."

As they danced away a skinny boy tried to croon as much like Frank Sinatra as he resembled him. When he sang about old familiar places in "I'll be Seeing You" Kate's eyes filled with tears.

"Whoever the fellow is that you're thinking of," said Scrappy, "I hope he realizes what a lucky dog he is."

"How do you know I was thinking of a particular man?"

"I've been in the racket of observing people a long time. I'm never wrong."

"His name is Mike King. He's in the army."

"The son of the shoe store owner?"

"That's the fella."

Three songs later the band paused a beat, and a trio of girls replaced the skinny boy with their imitation of the Andrews Sisters' "Beer Barrel Polka." Scrappy let out a grunt. "It appears that's as far as my fifty bucks went."

As they left the dance floor, Beatrice Bradshaw rushed to greet them. "Such a charming couple you are. And what a dashing figure you cut, Mr. MacFarland."

"It's amazing what a couple of lessons at the Arthur Murray dance studio can achieve," he said. "While I'm handing out credits, Beatrice, you've done a fantastic job in organizing this soirée. And I have said so in an editorial that will appear in Monday's paper."

"Aren't you being a little hasty?" demanded Kate. "What if the evening flopped?"

"As editor in chief of a newspaper I get to say what's a success and what's a flop."

"First you claim to be flawless at analyzing people and

now you claim the right to render judgments when you have no facts to back them up. What a conceited fellow you are."

"There's a pot calling a kettle black! I seem to recall you boasting how good you are at getting to the bottom of things. What's that if not conceit?"

"I've never claimed to be able to look at a person and read what's going on inside that person's mind."

"It's not a matter of mind reading, Kate. It's intuition. Everybody has it, although I'd say that in your case it's more highly developed."

"Why am I so special?"

"Simply because you're a firstborn. In my experience the eldest child is always more intuitively developed. I call it the Big Brother/Big Sister syndrome. However, in a large family it's also a phenomenon found in the youngest child, though never to the same degree. That is what accounts for the special relationship that's almost always seen between the oldest and youngest in a big family such as yours."

Having listened intently, Beatrice interjected, "You *are* close to Paulie, Kate."

"My little brother has been called a lot of things," she said with a little laugh, "but this is the first time I've heard Paulie described as intuitive. Or myself."

"If not intuition," said Scrappy, "to what would you account your steadfast insistence, without an iota of evidence, that Freddy Johnson is innocent?"

"That's easy. I've known Freddy since we were in the first grade."

"I couldn't estimate how many times I've covered a

murder in which someone said of the guy who did it, 'I can't believe it. He was always such a nice boy.' "

"I *know* Freddy's not capable of doing such a terrible thing," Kate insisted.

"I'm sure his lawyer will be delighted to call on you as a witness to Freddy's upstanding character. But it would be even better if you could also provide the kid an alibi. According to information I've gotten from a reliable source close to the investigation, he doesn't have one. In fact there's a witness who saw Freddy arguing with Nancy last Saturday morning outside the Vale-Rio Diner."

"That proves nothing. They had a date for breakfast. They were going to make up."

"Did they?"

"How should I know? And who was this mysterious eyewitness to their alleged fight?"

Scrappy shrugged and smiled. "I'm afraid I'm not able to share that information with you ladies at this time."

"Are you saving it so the *Independence* will score a scoop?"

"I'm saving it until I can confirm the witness's account. I was hoping to do so tonight," he said, looking around, "but he doesn't appear to be present."

"Ah-ha," Kate said. "This supposed witness is a man."

Scrappy barked a laugh. "That's very good, Kate! You are good at getting to the bottom of things. All you have to do now is figure out which man had a reason to be in the vicinity of the Vale-Rio at that early hour last Saturday morning."

"Has it occurred to you and the police that this man might be the killer?"

"I don't know if it's occurred to the police. It has to me, but I doubt he's the killer."

"If you haven't spoken to him, how can you dismiss him as a suspect? *Intuition?*

"The man has a plausible reason to have been there at the time. And then there is the question of motive. We know this was not a sex crime. And because Nancy had money in her purse and was found wearing a ring and a necklace, it wasn't robbery. Finally, it seems likely that Nancy knew her killer and went out to the lonely spot with him willingly. All indications are that this wasn't an abduction. In view of what the witness has said, all of that makes it look bad for Freddy Johnson."

"This is nothing but circumstantial evidence!"

"Since eyewitnesses to murders are exceedingly rare, the vast majority of murderers are convicted on circumstantial evidence."

"Do you believe Freddy did it?"

"I'm a newspaperman. I deal in facts. What I *believe* is immaterial."

Looking round the gymnasium, Kate found Chief Detwiler standing with Jim Kerner by a bar offering fruit punch. "Just because the police *say* someone is guilty," she said, "Scrappy MacFarland is willing to accept their word?"

"My job is to *report*," he replied gruffly. "Whether their word is to be believed is up to the twelve men on the jury who will listen to them, examine the evidence, and follow the law as a judge explains it."

"And a fine system it is," Beatrice declared with an emphatic nod of her head. "But may I suggest that we set aside all this talk about murder and try having a good time?"

"An excellent idea, Beatrice," said Scrappy. "I'm going to slip the bandleader five bucks to play a waltz and then have a whirl around the floor with the most charming lady in the joint."

"Oh please, Scrappy," Kate pleaded. "I'm not ready for another dance."

"Glad to hear it," he said, walking away, "because I was referring to Beatrice."

9

SHORTLY BEFORE ONE o'clock, an hour after the Robinsville High School Swing Band signaled the end of the V-for-Victory Rally and Dance by playing "Goodnight Sweetheart," Officer Todd Doebling began a fourth and last survey of downtown. Judging by the number of people he had observed throughout the evening along Bridge Street, the gala at the junior high school had not caused a serious dent in Saturday night shopping. Moviegoers had also been out, lining up for both shows of the Colonial's new feature, *Woman of the Year*, starring Spencer Tracy and Katharine Hepburn. Families had turned out for dinner pretty much as usual. At midnight as many drinkers as he would have expected on any Saturday left bars which Sunday Blue Laws required to close at twelve o'clock. He had made no arrests, issued no warnings to rambunctious youths, ordered no one to move along, and written no citations for traffic violations.

Turning from Bridge Street for the second time during his shift to survey the security of the windows and doors of the small factories on Canal Street he saw smoke.

Two minutes later, Scrappy MacFarland heard the Klaxon on the roof of the rolling mill summoning volunteer fire companies. This was accomplished by a series of blasts which corresponded to the numbers on a grid map of the town. If the Klaxon sounded the number repeatedly, the fire was a very large one.

When the number thirty-four blared four times, it was, as far as Scrappy could recall while he searched for a copy of the grid map, unprecedented. But before he could consult it the telephone atop his bedside table rang. "Mr. MacFarland, sorry to bother you at home so late," said Toby Jackson, the nightman at the paper, "but I thought you would want to know there's a huge fire on Canal Street."

"What's burning?"

"The Gordon furniture factory."

"I'm on my way. See how many of our people you can roust and tell 'em to get down there fast. Then grab a press Graphic camera for me and meet me at the scene."

Watching his company go up in flames, Stanley Gordon sobbed, "Everything was going so well for the business! After we managed to hang on during the Depression, we were just starting to get back on our feet."

"It is a terrible loss," Scrappy said, "But thank goodness it happened when nobody was inside working."

"But there was," Gordon exclaimed. "The night

watchman. Oh my lord, I hope and pray Jonas got out safely."

Despite a two-hour struggle to bring the conflagration under control, the presence of so much wood, paint, varnish, lacquers, and other flammables in the plant had prevented twenty gallant firemen from saving the factory.

Only after the fire was officially declared out by Volunteer Fire Chief Ed Majors was a squad of men permitted to venture into the smoldering ruins. While the men looked for hotspots that might flare up and require more fighting, the body was found.

A mile away, on the west side of town, awakened by sirens, Paulie Fallon had scrambled from bed to the window of the back bedroom he had shared with his brother before Jack went into the navy. He wished this fire was as near as the last big one, four years ago, when Farnum's cookie bakery burned down. Only half a mile away, its flames had been so close he had felt the heat on the window glass. And the air had smelled like chocolate.

What a night!

The only bad thing about it was that the cookie factory had to close and Jack lost his part-time, after-school job as stock boy. This meant he could no longer bring home big bags of cookies rejected by inspectors because they were broken.

This fire was farther away and produced only a red glow in the sky. Gazing at it, Paulie had imagined that the B-17 bomber now parked atop his bureau had dropped its bomb load squarely on a Panzer tank factory somewhere deep in Nazi Germany. Long since safely back at base, the crew of the plane awaited orders for its next mission from pilot Colonel Paul Fallon. As a result of the success of the air raid, he was to be decorated by the Army Air Corps and promoted to Brigadier General. The ceremony would be held immediately after he had brought a bucket of coal up to the kitchen from the bin in the cellar. In the meantime, because the glow from the distant fire was fading, there was nothing to do but go to sleep.

Eight hours later, alert to the smells of coffee brewing and toasting bread, he waited for his mother to yell upstairs for him to get out of bed this very instant and come down immediately or go hungry because she wasn't running a restaurant.

In the next room the radio was tuned to a program of music, and Kate was singing along with Dinah Shore to a sappy tune that only a girl could like. Called "Happiness Is a Thing Called Joe," it was changed by Kate to "Happiness Is a Thing Called Mike."

Lying on his side and gazing across the room at the B-17, he heard the telephone ring and then his mother shout up the stairs, "Kate, it's for you."

This was followed by, "Paulie, get out of bed now. The coal bucket's empty. Your dad will be home any minute. So get a move on. I am not running a restaurant."

Coming downstairs, he heard Kate speaking on the phone in the parlor but could not make out what she was saying.

As she entered the kitchen a few moments later, she looked pale as a ghost. "That was Mrs. Bee. She said the fire last night was at Gordon's." She sighed. "That means I'm out of a job."

10

FOR YEARS, THE owner of Ed Polansky's music store on Bridge Street had been putting up with a joke about his other, original, and continuing profession.

The joke was in the form of a question and answer:

> *"Why is Ed Polanksy a reliable person?"*
> *"Everything he undertakes he carries out."*

Of course, no one had ever cracked wise about what Ed had trained to do for a living when the time came to deal with the democracy of death. Rich, poor, or somewhere between, sooner or later, ready or not, no one escaped the inevitable leveling that awaited them in the basement of Polansky's funeral home in a big brick house at the corner of Manavon Street and First Avenue.

Proving the point on this Sunday morning were two

men who could not have been more different, living or dead.

Ready to be laid out for the viewing scheduled for Monday evening, Lester Webber had dropped dead of a heart attack six years past the biblical allotment of fourscore and ten. Retired after a busy life as proprietor of a men's clothing store on Gay Street and renowned for having never missed a game, whether at home or away, of the Robinsville High School Phantoms football team, he had left a will establishing an annual scholarship for an athlete with the capability of going to college, but not the funds. The will had created an endowment of one hundred thousand dollars. Mr. Webber had also bequeathed his widow, a daughter, three sons, and seven grandchildren an estate estimated in the *Independence* obituary at close to half a million dollars. The eulogy at First Presbyterian Church would be delivered by Mayor Cantrell. To escort the procession of fifteen automobiles, the Cadillac hearse, and three Chrysler floral vehicles through the downtown streets to a cemetery on the north side, Chief of Police Detwiler had assigned three of the town's four patrol cars.

Befitting this respectable citizen, the Webber family had selected a top-of-the-line mahogany casket with satin lining and silver fittings to be carried by six strapping white-gloved pallbearers, each a Phantoms football letterman. The honorary bearers would be the chief, mayor, school-board president, and the town's second most ardent Phantoms fan, Scrappy MacFarland.

The second cadaver, lying naked on its back on a stainless-steel table, had been so badly charred by the fire that ripped through Gordon's furniture factory that he had been identified only because his leather wallet survived the blaze. It contained four dollars, a driver's license, and a card issued by the draft board certifying that twenty-six-year-old Jonas Longacre had been classified 4-F, having been deemed medically unfit for military service because of acute alcoholism.

Known by everyone in town as a ne'er-do-well with no family, Jonas had found employment as Gordon's weekend nightwatchman only because Stanley Gordon was a gentleman who believed being Christian required more than being present in church on Sunday. Even before Jonas's body was brought to the funeral home, Stanley had been on the phone asking Ed to provide Jonas a decent burial and to forward the bill to the company's accountant.

Despite these differences in their lives and the circumstances of their deaths, Lester Webber and Jonas Longacre found commonality under the law. Neither died in the presence of a physician, and so before a death certificate could be issued, official cause had to be determined by autopsy.

Lester Webber's provided no surprises. Cause of death was entered on the certificate as coronary occlusion as the result of advanced arteriosclerosis.

Having autopsied other victims of fire, Ed did not expect to find that Jonas Longacre had actually burned to death. As he began the examination, he anticipated immediate evidence of death by asphyxiation resulting from inhalation of the deadly toxins and noxious gases found in smoke.

Yet Jonas's lungs offered nothing in the way of such

damage beyond that found in an individual who was known to smoke three packs of cigarettes a day as he did.

Suspending the autopsy, Ed picked up the telephone and dialed the home number of Chief Detwiler.

After hours spent at the fire, Detwiler answered the call sounding tired and grumpy.

"Sorry to disturb you, Tom," Ed said, "but I found something odd in the autopsy of Jonas Longacre."

"Such as what?"

"Such as the fact that he did not die in that fire."

"Come on, Ed. Of course he did. That body was practically burnt to a crisp."

"He was certainly severely burned. But there is evidence he was already dead sometime before the fire started."

"Then how the hell did he die?"

"I don't know yet. But before I continue, I think it best that you be present. You could be dealing with a crime."

"I'll be there in ten."

Six minutes after Detwiler arrived, Ed removed Longacre's scorched scalp to reveal the skull and a bullet hole.

11

BECAUSE SCRAPPY MACFARLAND did not receive the call from Ed Polansky until after eleven o'clock Sunday night, over an hour after Monday's edition of the *Independence* had been put to bed, the paper could not tell its readers of the second murder in the town in eight days until the Tuesday edition. All they would find in Monday's paper was that a body found in the ruins of Gordon's factory had been *tentatively* identified as Jonas Longacre. By then, however, Robinsville's gossip grapevine would certainly be buzzing with talk of the shocker.

Consequently, when Mrs. Mary Edinger left her house a few minutes before nine o'clock to go next door to visit Beatrice Bradshaw, a rumor that Ed Polansky had found a bullet hole in Jonas Longacre's head had reached her by way of a series of phone calls culminating in one from Cora Baxter.

While Cora was on the phone with Mary, four blocks from Mrs. Edinger's house Kate Fallon awoke at her usual hour and realized with a sinking feeling in her stomach that for the first time in the nearly eight years since she'd graduated from high school she had no job to go to. Entering the kitchen, she found her mother washing dishes used by Paulie before he went off to school with soaring expectations of making his classmates jealous with his toy B-17.

Without looking up from the sink, Mrs. Fallon asked Kate, "What would you like for breakfast?"

Giving her a hug, Kate said, "I'm afraid I'm not in the mood for breakfast, Mom. I thought I'd drop in on Mrs. Bee for a cup of coffee."

After two knocks on Beatrice's kitchen door, Kate walked in and found her friend and Mrs. Edinger at the table.

Except during Beatrice's sojourns to New York City, once in summer and once in winter, Mary had popped in each Monday through Friday, arriving just in time for Don McNeill and the rest of his radio family on *The Breakfast Club*. He always started the program with, "Good morning, breakfast clubbers, good morning to yah. We got up bright and early, just to how-dee-do-yah."

With cups of coffee and the scrumptious little scones Beatrice always served with thick clotted cream and jam, Mary would spend the hour with her neighbor before Beatrice had to leave to open the Book Nook for the day. And how time would fly as they chuckled at the happy banter between Don and Fran Allison as Aunt Fanny, a dispenser of zany, down-home gossip. At some point there came a rowdy moment in which the band played rousingly and Don coaxed radio listeners to "march around the breakfast table."

In the part of the program Mary liked most Don said, "Each in his own words and each in his own way, for a world united in peace, bow your heads and let us pray." Then she silently asked God to help America win the war and to bless her late husband William and her murdered daughter Nancy. She ended with thanks to the Almighty for the lovely, generous woman who not once in all the years as her neighbor failed to welcome her with seemingly boundless cheer as Don McNeill was signing off his program.

Rising to embrace Kate, Beatrice said, "I am so sorry about what's happened, my dear. I know how much you enjoyed working at Gordon's. But I'm sure a young woman with your talent and your experience will soon find another place to work. I wish I were in a position to hire you at the store."

"I'm afraid you wouldn't get much work out of me," Kate said, as Beatrice turned away to pour Kate a cup of coffee. "I'd spend all my time reading."

"It is my settled opinion that hours spent reading," Beatrice said, carrying the cup to the table, "are added by God to the span of one's lifetime."

"If that's true," Kate said, sipping, "I'll live to be a very old woman."

Delicately setting down her coffee cup, Mrs. Edinger excused herself for home and quietly left through the back door.

"How is she doing?" Kate asked quietly.

Beatrice shook her head sadly. Then, quite suddenly, her eyes opened wide. "Dear, I almost forgot," she said excitedly, "Kate, have you heard the terrible news about your old classmate Jonas Longacre?"

Kate sighed. "Oh my. What's he done now?"

Beatrice leaned very close. "They found him dead in the fire."

"Oh my gosh, that's horrible. Poor Jonas."

"Yes, but that's not all," said Beatrice. "After they took the body to Polansky's funeral home, Ed found a bullet hole." Rearing back, she tapped a finger to her right temple. "In the head.

"I mean, I always knew Jonas was troubled," Beatrice continued, "but he never struck me as someone who would shoot himself."

Kate blurted, "Maybe he didn't."

Beatrice blinked. "What ever could you mean?"

"What if somebody else shot him and then started that fire so nobody would suspect it was a murder?"

Beatrice responded with a derisive chuckle. "Why on earth would anyone wish to murder a harmless inebriate? Now, if it was his boss Stanley Gordon whose body was found with a bullet hole in him, you might have reason to suspect murder. But why Jonas? That sort of thing happens only in mystery novels."

"Now, let's talk about something more pleasant, dear," Beatrice said. "Why Mary was just saying that her niece Virginia, who lives up in Long Island, has been hired by the Grumman aviation company to help build airplanes. Mary said to her, 'Ginny, what do you know about airplanes?' And she said they will teach her all she needs to know. Of course, she's not really building a whole airplane. She rivets parts to wings. I told Mary I wouldn't want to go zipping around in the skies on wings she made. I was joking, naturally. Mary says that Ginny's always been very good at making things. And I read an article in the *Bulletin* that a lot of jobs at the Philadelphia shipyards are being taken over by women because the men are being drafted.

"It's not just shipyards who are losing men," Beatrice went on. "I was talking to Dotty Smith in the store the other day and she told me that the Manyon company lost four welders in the past month because two were drafted and the others enlisted. There's an idea for you, Kate. Put in an application at Manyon's."

Kate pressed a hand to her chest. "Me? I don't know a darn thing about welding."

"You're smart. You'll learn. Men do, why not *you*?"

Kate looked into her cup. "What would Mike think if I wrote and told him I'd taken up *welding*?"

"Your fiancé is a sweet young man," said Beatrice, "but did he ask you what you thought about his going into law?"

"That was different."

"What was the difference?"

"He's a man."

"Yes he is. And God bless him. But at the moment, Manyon's Precision Metals is short of men, there is a war to be won, and you are unemployed. Besides, if you decide you don't like it, you can quit. As to Mike, I see no reason whatsoever why he needs to know about it until you've made up your mind."

Kate thought a moment. Feeling tears welling, she said, "It would be nice if I could do work that might in some way speed the end of the war so Mike could come home and we could finally begin our lives together."

Pushing away from the table, Beatrice declared, "There is your answer, Kate. Now, if you'll excuse me, I do have a bookstore to run."

Returning home, Kate found a letter from Mike in the morning's mail delivery.

Opening it in her bedroom, she read:

Hi sweetheart!

This is going to be short. We're on a fifteen-minute break before we head out to the firing range. I'm getting to be really good with the M-1 rifle. Of course, I don't expect to be called on to use one after the war is over! I may not even get a chance to shoot Nazis or Japs with it. The captain of our training company has informed me that he will be recommending me for officers' school. He thinks it would be a terrible waste of manpower if I went into the infantry. He says I belong in a staff job. As they say on the radio, "Stay tuned."

How much I miss you! What I would give to take you in my arms right now and smother you with kisses.

There's the top sergeant's whistle. Got to go. Love to all. Tell Paulie I haven't forgotten that he wants a Nazi flag as a souvenir.

All my love, love, love, love, love, always. Mike

P.S. Write back soon!

Sitting at her dressing table, Kate wrote:

My darling,

I think it's wonderful that your captain thinks you should be an officer. With your brains, this awful war would be ended quickly and you could be in my arms where you belong. If only I could be with you, even for a minute! But since I can't, I will try to make this letter as much like your being with me as I can.

I just came from visiting Mrs. Bee at her house. She said that Mrs. Edinger's niece is working in a factory on Long Island that makes airplanes. In case you didn't know, because of the war a lot of women have taken over factory jobs that used to be done by men. The reason the subject came up is that there was a fire Saturday night at Gordon's.

I'm sure you remember Jonas Longacre. Lately, he was working at Gordon's as night watchman on weekends. I'm sorry to tell you that he was killed in the fire.

I'm also sorry to say the entire factory burned down, which means I'm now out of work.

Mrs. Bee thinks I should apply for one of the jobs left open at Manyon's metal company. It seems that four of the welders went into the service, and Mr. Manyon is looking for people to take over for them. I have no idea if he would hire a woman or how long it might take him to fill the positions, so if I am going to put in an application, I'll have to do so pretty quickly. I suppose a welder would be paid more than

I was earning as a typist at Gordon's, which would be nice. I also feel that I'd be contributing to the war effort. Can you imagine me in overalls? Ha-ha!

The other news I have for you is that the V-for-Victory Rally and Dance was a huge success and a lot of fun. I even danced! Don't worry, though! I danced with Scrappy MacFarland. For such a large man, he was very light on his feet and didn't step on mine once. But I was wishing the whole time that it was you dancing with me. When the band played "I'll Be Seeing You" I almost broke down and cried because I miss you so deeply.

I will tell Paulie that you haven't forgotten his Nazi flag souvenir. Right now he is very much occupied with a toy B-17 bomber that he bought at Woolworth's. Mom and Dad send their love, as does Mrs. Bee.

Your adoring fianceé.

P.S. Mrs. Bee says she heard that when Jonas's body was examined by Ed Polansky that he found a bullet hole in Jonas's head. Can you believe we may have had yet another murder here?

That evening at supper, with all the nonchalance she could muster, she said, "What with the war and all, and with so many boys being called up to fight in it, the Manyon Precision Metal Company is very short of welders."

"Shortage of manpower," said her father as he reached past Paulie for a bowl of boiled potatoes. "It's a serious problem for industries everywhere."

"Exactly," she said emphatically. "That's why, since I have no job at Gordon's anymore, I'm giving some thought to putting in an application at Manyon's."

Thomas Fallon's callused hand hovered above the white bowl. "I beg your pardon? You're thinking of doing what?"

Eyes around the table widened in anticipation.

"I see no value whatsoever to the war effort," Kate said, "in me looking for another job that will have me typing more of the meaningless memos and letters I typed at Gordon's. If I were a welder, I'd be contributing to victory in the war."

With a jerk of his head and the scoffing smirk of a twelve-year-old, Paulie blurted, "What's a *girl* know about *welding*?"

Thomas Fallon lifted the bowl with one hand and fanned the air with the other as if shooing a fly. "No daughter of mine is going to be like the girl in that Norman Rockwell picture on the cover of the *Saturday Evening Post*, her arms bulging with big muscles like an Amazon."

Arlene giggled. "My sister the Amazon!"

With a look that commanded silence, Thomas Fallon continued, "For once, Kate, your brother is right. Welding is not a proper job for a young woman."

12

RESPONDING TO A report of a prowler in the backyard of the Murray house on Brookview Avenue, Officer Todd Doebling looked sidelong at Probationary Officer Mickey Ludlum. "I will bet you dollars to doughnuts this is a false alarm."

"Why do you say that?"

"Monday night, *Inner Sanctum* is on the radio."

"So what?"

"It's a scary show, and sometimes the old lady gets carried away and imagines prowlers."

"Maybe this time she actually spotted someone."

A few minutes later they found the frail elderly woman on a curving flagstone walk leading to the large old stone-and-brick house with lights on in every window. "I was listening to the radio in my bedroom at the back of the house," she said, "and my collie started barking.

When I looked out the window I saw a man. He was sneaking through the yard."

Doebling asked, "Can you describe him for us?"

"All I saw was a shadow going toward Mr. Bohannon's house from the direction of Mrs. Bradshaw's. When I turned on the light at the back porch to get a better look at him he was gone."

With a half smile at Ludlum, Doebling said, "Miss Murray, might I make a suggestion?"

"Please do."

"Since you have a light on your back porch, why not keep it on at night? Prowlers don't go sneaking around in places where there are lights."

"I used to keep it lit all the time," she said, "but since the government asked everybody to cut back on the electricity, I stopped doing it."

"That's very patriotic of you, but I'm sure it will be all right if you turn it on again. The bulb you use doesn't have to be a bright one that burns up a lot of electricity. Get yourself a small one. Fifteen watts at the most will do the trick. And just to make sure you don't get in hot water with the government, I'll file a report with the Office of Civilian Defense, Department of Special Permissions, stating the police have told you it's okay. Of course, you will still have to turn it off in a blackout. But that will be okay. Prowlers don't go out during blackouts."

The elderly woman's eyes went wide. "Really, Officer?"

"Oh yes indeed. They wouldn't dare. It's just too risky, on account of there being so many air-raid wardens keeping watch all over town."

"I will certainly take your advice. Thank you."

"It's quite all right," Doebling said. "You have a pleasant night now."

Back in the car, Ludlum laughed. "Office of Civil Defense, Department of Special Permissions! What a crock of bull!"

"Yeah, well maybe now we'll stop getting groundless calls," Doebling said, turning the car from Brookview into Manavon Street in the direction of Polanksy's funeral home. As they passed, Doebling surveyed a cluster of middle-aged men. Having paid their respects to the laid-out body of Lester Webber, they lingered on the front sidewalk as smoke from their cigarettes and cigars hovered ghostlike over their heads.

Having attended the viewing as both an old friend of Webber and reporter of the event for the *Independence*, Scrappy MacFarland had returned to the newspaper's office to bat out a brief story with a hunt-and-peck typing system of lightning speed and paucity of errors that left the other reporters envious and the linotypists grateful.

Had final obsequies for a pillar of Robinsville's commercial and social circles been held on any other night, Scrappy mused as he handed the story to a copyboy to take down to the composing room, it would have been Tuesday's main headline. But that honor had been trumped by Ed Polanksy's discovery of a bullet hole in the body found amongst the smoldering rubble of the furniture factory. The story provided all the elements. It offered shock value, a well-known resident of disreputable character who had been taken under the wing of one of the town's upstanding citizens, and a murder under such mysterious circumstances it could have been the plot for a *Thin Man* movie starring William Powell as dapper detective Nick Charles, or perhaps another Dashiell Hammett tale featuring hard-boiled sleuth Sam Spade.

The murder of Jonas Longacre demanded the dominant place on Tuesday's front page not only because it was a sensational story, but because it was *local*. Had the same circumstances happened in Philadelphia, or even as close as Norristown, the story *might* be a one-line item in "Other News" on an inside page.

To demonstrate the ascendency of local news he had devised for the benefit of journalistic novices "MacFarland's Newsworthiness Equivalency Guide." Tacked onto a wall behind his desk, it decreed:

200,000 Filipinos missing after typhoon =

4,000 Peruvian peasants lost in an earthquake =

540 Chinese drowned as overloaded ferry sinks =

102 workers trapped in Welsh coal-mine explosion =

40 retirees killed in Florida old-age home fire =

5 unsolved burglaries of a downtown store.

None of these, however, matched the murder of a pretty hometown girl.

Local angle notwithstanding, just how long Jonas Longacre continued to occupy page-one space depended on how quickly Chief Detwiler's police force solved this murder. Would it, like the killing of the Griffith woman two months ago, remain unsolved? Or might there be, he thought as he drove toward a breakfast at the Vale-Rio Diner, as swift a resolution as the one that seemed to be in the offing in the Edinger homicide? Assuming, that is, that Freddy Johnson was still the only suspect.

13

A S THE LAST of the tangy scrapple went into Scrappy's mouth at the Vale-Rio, Kate Fallon entered her mother's kitchen dressed in a navy blue coat over a gray skirt and white blouse. Finding her brother in a red-and-blue-plaid flannel shirt and dungarees, she marveled at how much he resembled their uncle Harry. Alone and eating a bowl of Wheaties, he peered at her quizzically, and said, "You're good at figuring who done it in all those mystery books you're always reading. Who do you think killed that guy where you worked?"

Opening the refrigerator in the hope of finding orange juice and being disappointed, she snapped, "How on earth would I know?"

Paulie poked the soggy cereal with a spoon. "You don't have to bite my head off."

"I'm sorry," Kate said, taking out a full bottle of milk. "I'm a little on edge this morning."

"Where are you going all dolled up?"

Kate poured a half a glass of milk. "None of your business. Finish your breakfast or you'll be late for school."

Through a mouthful of Wheaties, Paulie said. "Bet I know."

Looking with dismay at a droplet of milk dribbling down his chin, she said, "Don't talk with food in your mouth."

Wiping away the milk with a sleeve, he said, "You're going to Manyon's about a welding job."

Frowning, Kate asked, "Where's Mom?"

"She went next door to Mrs. Hartzel's to see about borrowing a cup of flour until she can go to the store tomorrow. You know what that means."

Kate finished the milk. "I'm afraid I don't."

"It means meat pie for tonight's supper."

"Good," she said, wiping away a milk mustache with her napkin. "I happen to like Mom's meat pie."

Scooping out the last of the cereal, Paulie said, "Do you think they'll catch whoever shot that guy?"

"If you've finished, go to school."

"In case you do get the welding job," he said, leaving the bowl on the table, "I hope you won't work the night shift."

"What difference does it make what shift I work?"

He paused at the kitchen door. "If you work nights, who will take me to movies Friday nights at the Rialto?"

"I'm sure Arlene will be happy to take you."

"Maybe, but going with her is no fun 'cause she only lets me have one box of Good & Plenty. And she doesn't like to take me if it's a Frankenstein or mummy picture. And she won't let me sit way down in front the way you do."

As the door closed, Kate took her glass along with Paulie's bowl and spoon and placed them in the sink with other dirty dishes. Starting to wash them, she heard her mother's voice.

"Leave them be," she said, carrying a heaping measuring cup of flour. "You'll mess up your clothes. I'll wash them after I'm done baking. How come you're dressed to the nines this morning?"

"I thought I'd see if I can get myself a meaningful job."

With a worried look, Mrs. Fallon placed the cup of flour on the table. "You know how your father feels about you taking a job in a factory, Kate. He made that very clear at supper."

"How would you feel about it, Mom?"

"How I feel is not important."

"It is to me."

"There must be other places for you to work that are a lot closer than Manyon's. You could walk to Gordon's. The Manyon plant is three miles out of town."

"Yes, but the Bridge Street bus goes right to the door. How far I have to go is not the point. I want to feel useful. I need to know that I am doing work that will help end the war and bring Mike and Jack home. If Dad were in the army or navy, you'd want to do everything you could to hurry him back to you."

"If you get a job in a factory, he's going to be very upset."

"I've upset him plenty of times, and he soon got over it."

"Well, it's your life! I've no wish to run it for you. Now leave the dishes and run along. I have a meat pie to make."

Standing by the door, Kate looked back at her mother. "All this worry about how Dad might feel could turn out to be unnecessary. Mr. Manyon might agree with Dad that a factory is no place for a woman to work."

A few minutes later, boarding the bus, she was shocked to find herself greeted with whistles from several young men in heavy, long, olive green army overcoats or short field jackets. Assuming they were heading to the new hospital site and that many more like them were soon to follow, she decided that if the worst thing to happen during the war was being whistled at, the only way to react was to appear neither flattered, embarrassed, nor angry, but coolly indifferent. Thinking ahead and picturing herself getting on the bus in welders' coveralls, she hoped she would subsequently be seen by the soldiers as not just a young woman, but an American who was, like them, working hard to win the war.

After slowly climbing a long hill, the bus crossed the town line and slowed to allow three green-and-white Trainer's Dairy trucks to make a turn as they came back from predawn delivery runs. Picking up speed, the bus skirted wintry farmland and clusters of woods where not so very long ago Mike King and Jack Fallon went gunning for deer, although never successfully. Recalling Mike's boast in his letter that he was becoming an expert with an M-1 rifle, Kate thought it ironic that an outcome of the war, besides the defeat of tyrannies, might be a steady supply of venison.

When the bus stopped in front of the sign identifying

the site of the Indian Creek U.S. Army Hospital and the soldiers got off silently, she looked through the window and marveled that so much work had been done already. Between ranks of cantaloupe-colored, two-story wood barracks, roads had been laid out and paved with asphalt. Where Mike and Jack had fruitlessly stalked deer stood several large redbrick buildings with signs affixed, designating them as future hospital wards. Beyond them a chain-link fence separated the army property from the dirt lane beside Indian Creek where two boys toting fishing poles had made a discovery which resulted in Freddy Johnson being named the prime suspect in a murder investigation.

Now, as the bus pulled away from the site of the murder, she shook her head and whispered to herself, "Ridiculous!"

A few moments later, the bus driver shouted, "Last stop, miss."

14

JEROME MANYON, A short man with snow-white hair and wearing a gray double-breasted suit, smiled across a paper-strewn desk. "Please have a seat, Miss Fallon. I've been expecting you."

With a quizzical look she sat in a brown-leather wing chair. "You have?"

"I had a call about you," Manyon said, grinning and making a steeple of his hands beneath his chin. "Beatrice Bradshaw phoned yesterday afternoon to tell me you might be coming out to see me about a job. Obviously, Miss Fallon, you are not a woman to let grass grow under her feet. I like gals who show initiative."

"Being suddenly out of a job does focus one's attention."

The hands folded and settled upon the desk as though he were a schoolboy. "What a tragedy that fire was for poor Stan. The man worked so hard to make something of that business, only to have it go up in flames in a few minutes. And then to be told that it could have been started to cover up the murder of one of his workers! What is this world coming to when something like that can happen in a quiet little town like ours? I was saying to Mr. MacFarland last night at Lester's viewing that the whole world seems to have gone haywire. And to have such an occurrence on the same night as the V-for-Victory dance!"

Relaxing, Kate said, "Did you and Mrs. Manyon attend?"

"Alas, Mrs. Manyon passed away two years ago."

"I'm sorry."

"She had a good life. I'm sure if she had lived to see the day that a woman came in applying for a job here she would have been thrilled to pieces. She's probably looking down at me from Heaven right now, so I had better get down to business and tell you what to expect when you come to work here."

"Excuse me, Mr. Manyon," Kate said, coming up straight. "You said *when*. Don't you mean *if*?"

The hands unfolded and flattened atop the desk. "Well, of course, I do not expect you to decide right now. But I do have three openings, and from everything Bea Bradshaw had to say about you, I see no reason why you shouldn't fill one of them."

Kate smiled nervously. "I thought I'd probably have to take some kind of aptitude test."

"The best test I know of for judging aptitude is observing a person's attitude. Yours is impressively positive. Everything you need to know, you'll be taught on the job."

"I'll do my best not to let you down, sir. And Mrs. Bee."

"Now, let me tell you what we do at Manyon Precision Metals. Before the war we manufactured parts for makers of household equipment. Vacuum cleaners, floor waxers, and the like. Now we've got housing subcontracts for anti-tank guns, machine-guns mounts, and settings for bomb sights. At one stage or another all of these require some spot welding. That's what you will be trained to do, spot welding. I hope you've got good eyesight.

"Twenty-twenty."

"I don't mean to be impertinent with this next question," he said, drumming fingers on the desk. "Are you a drinker?"

"If I go out for a dinner I might have a glass of wine."

"I usually have two myself. And a martini before. But you know what I was getting at."

"I am not a boozer."

Hands folded once more, he asked, "How long did you work for Stan Gordon?"

"Seven and a half years. Since I graduated from high school.

Pale blue eyes studied her intently. "I suppose you'd better do something about your hair."

Kate self-consciously primped it. "What's wrong with it?"

"Much too long. We wouldn't want it caught in machinery, or set on fire by a spark, would we?"

Kate laughed. "No, we certainly wouldn't."

"I'm not an expert on women's hairdos, but maybe you

could cut it shorter. Or put it up in braids. I always liked braids. My late wife wore braids sometimes. How about a bun? No, I know just the right thing. My wife used to wear one gardening. You might get one of those things, those hair nets.

"As to what clothes you will wear, the company will provide you coveralls. They're not exactly chick, or however that word is pronounced. You know, c-h-i-c."

"I believe it's *sheek*."

"Now as to pay, my wife always preached that if a woman does a man's work she should receive the same wages. You'll get what the men earn. That's sixty cents an hour. This could be a bone of contention between the union and me. Until now the only women on the payroll work in the office. Until I can hammer the issue out with the union committee, you'll be carried on the rolls as an apprentice. The hours will be eight to four, Monday to Friday. But once you're trained, because you'll be lowest in seniority, you could get bumped to a night shift."

Kate nodded. "That's only fair."

"Today's Tuesday. Can you start next Monday?"

"I'm ready to start tomorrow."

"Monday will give me the time I'll need to work all this out with the union, and for the men to start to get used to the idea of working with a woman. A few may try to give you a hard time."

"I've got two brothers who have been giving me a hard time most of their lives. And then there's my fiancé, Mike King. He's never been one to let me get away with anything."

"Is that the King family with the shoe store?"

"That's right. Mike is in the army."

Manyon slapped a hand on the desk. "Shoes! I hope you have a pair or two in your closet without high heels."

"All my shoes are flats. You see, my fiancé is only an inch taller than I am, so—"

Manyon cut her off with a barked laugh. "No need to explain. Mrs. Manyon used to say that there is no cleverer creature on all of God's good green earth than a woman who recognizes there is no one vainer than a short man. Will I see you here bright and early Monday morning?"

Standing and extending a hand to him, Kate said, "Yes sir!"

Seated at the front of the Robinsville bus when it stopped at the army-hospital site, she was acutely aware of a handful of army privates who boarded with appraising looks at her. But as they began to take seats around her, an older man with captain's bars on the shoulders of his overcoat stepped on.

After a quick assessment, he commanded, "All right, you men, since we're all going to the last stop at the railroad station, I expect you to be gentlemen, make it easy for civilians who'll be getting on and off before us by taking seats in the back." As the men moved grudgingly, he smiled at Kate, and whispered, "My apologies for the men, miss. They're on their way to being good soldiers, but they still have a lot to learn about the responsibilities that go with wearing the uniform of their country."

Kate smiled. "I'm sure we civilians have a great deal of learning to do as well."

As the captain snapped a smart salute and followed his men to the rear and the bus lumbered away from the construction site, Kate tried to envision what Mike might be doing at that moment. She imagined how he was likely to feel once he received the letter telling him his fiancée had been hired as a welder.

When the bus stopped opposite Trainer's Dairy, Mr. Groover boarded. A burly, broad-shouldered, middle-aged man, he showed bounding energy at the end of each workday. His job began while Kate was still asleep and was nearly finished at seven o'clock when he delivered three quarts of milk to the Fallons' doorstep. With a surprised look, he said, "Miss Fallon, what an unexpected pleasure to find you on this bus. May I sit with you?"

"Of course. You'll probably be seeing a lot more of me on the bus," she said as he sat.

"I've only been taking it the past couple of weeks, because of the gasoline shortage. Why will you be riding it?"

"I start work at Manyon's on Monday."

"Congratulations."

"And to you on Johnny's scholarship to Notre Dame."

"What a relief. Without it, the kid would either be drafted or heading for a job on a labor gang at the steel plant. What'll you be doing at Manyon's? Secretarial and typing?"

"Because of the manpower shortage, Mr. Manyon is trying me out as a welder."

With an expression of astonishment and perhaps disapproval, Groover said. "A welder? That's . . . swell," and fell silent until his stop, where he said "Good luck with the job," and got off.

As the bus neared Pennsylvania Avenue, Kate chose to stay on all the way downtown and get off directly in front of Feicht's drugstore so she could buy a couple of hair nets. With the mission quickly accomplished and a small brown-paper bag tucked into her purse, she entered the Book Nook flushed with excitement.

"Oh, my dear Kate," exclaimed Beatrice, rushing to her, "I'm so glad you've come. I'm at my wit's end."

"What's wrong?"

"I'm worried about John Bohannon. I haven't seen him since the Victory Rally. I'd expected to see him at church Sunday. When I telephoned his home to see if he might be ill, I got no answer. I went around to his house this morning and he was not at home. I spoke to the neighbors, Mary Edinger and Eleanor Murray, and they told me they also have not seen him since Saturday. I phoned his home again today and still got no answer. All morning I've been trying to decide what to do. I thought of going to the police, but with what? An old woman's *hunch* that something *may* be wrong? With two murders on their hands, I'm afraid I'd get short shrift. Now, here you are to tell me what I should do."

"For whatever it's worth, somebody in a mystery novel, a detective, I'm sure, said that when you don't know what to do, it is wise to trust to inertia."

"It could have been said by Nero Wolfe," said Mrs. Bee. "Or it may have been Sherlock Holmes."

"Whoever said it, that's my advice," Kate said, affecting a comforting smile. "I'm sure Mr. Bohannon will show up with a very simple explanation."

Beatrice forced a slight smile. "I pray you're right. Now, what brings you to the Book Nook so early on a Tuesday?"

Beaming, Kate exclaimed, "I've landed a job."

"Oh, good for you. Where?"

"Thanks to your call to Mr. Manyon, I'm going to become a welder! I start training on Monday."

"That is wonderful news, my dear."

"But Monday seems so far off, I know I'm going to be on pins and needles the whole time."

"Then you must keep yourself busy."

"Easily said."

"In my experience, there is no better way to distract one's mind from worries than by reading. You're welcome to borrow all the titles you wish!"

Part 3

Everything That's Bright and Gay

15

ON FRIDAY AFTERNOON, with a glance at his Bulova wristwatch, Scrappy MacFarland drew one of two Phillies cigars from his shirt pocket, bit off the tip, sent it flying on a huff of breath, and bellowed across the city room, "All right, all you miserable ink-stained wretches, let's see about putting out a Saturday paper."

Posted to the wall of the city room of the Robinsville *Independence*, long yellow sheets of paper were arranged by category—War/Europe, War/Pacific, Washington, National, Foreign, State, Sports, Weather, Other. Below, a row of bulky black Associated Press and United Press International teletype machines chattered out news stories dated February 20, 1942, all of which left Scrappy feeling glum.

In Burma, the British Command acknowledged that Japanese troops were within reach of the railway which supplied the Burma Road, the lifeline to China and the army of Chiang Kai-Shek. And in the Philippines, General Douglas MacArthur reported that the trapped Americans at Bataan were being bombed almost constantly. Not far away a "fairly large convoy" of Japanese troop ships had arrived in Subic Bay. On the attack elsewhere in the Pacific, Japanese forces were engaged in combat with Americans in Java and Sumatra and the Japanese High Command in Tokyo was boasting that 73,000 British troops had been captured, including 8,000 wounded and 28 generals, in the capture of Singapore.

There was better news from Russia. If the report from Moscow could be believed, in eight months of fighting the Red Army had killed, wounded, or captured 6 million Germans, and knocked out or captured 15,000 tanks and 18,000 guns. *Pravda*, official newspaper of the Kremlin, claimed that 300,000 of those Germans had been killed between December 6 and January 15.

"One can only hope," Scrappy muttered. Turning his attention to the Washington paper, he read that the Senate and House passed resolutions for separate inquiries to determine whether sabotage or negligence caused the fire on the *Normandie*. Also passed in the House was a bill to spend $300,000 for the FBI to investigate activities of Japanese living on the West Coast. Included in the story was an item datelined San Francisco relating the FBI's arrest of 150 Japanese in central and Southern California and in the area around the Bonneville Dam in Oregon.

From the White House had come an item noting that President Roosevelt had issued an executive order permitting Secretary of War Henry L. Stimson to authorize the rounding up and removal of "any and all persons," particularly West Coast Japanese-Americans and aliens, as protection against sabotage.

A small item from the War Department noted that a reorganization of the Army General Staff had been completed with the appointment by General George C. Marshall of a new chief of the War Plans Division, a brigadier general Scrappy had never heard of by the name of Dwight D. Eisenhower.

Also taken down and carried to Scrappy's desk was an item from the nation's capital which he knew would be of more immediate interest to readers of his paper. As of March 16, it stated, the goverment would impose the rationing of sugar.

Lighting the cigar, Scrappy grumbled. "Attention grocery-store owners! Stand by for stampeding hoarders!"

Fifteen minutes later, bells ringing throughout the halls of Memorial Junior High School created a different sort of rush as school let out for the weekend. For Paulie Fallon this ordinarily meant two days of living life pretty much on his own terms.

This feeling of freedom started with not being expected to rush home right after school, so long as hanging out with friends at the Gateway soda shop did not make him late for his mother s customary Friday supper of oyster stew or fried oyster sandwiches at five o'clock.

Then it was *Jack Armstrong, All-American Boy*, on the radio at 5:30, followed by *Captain Midnight*, before his father took over the radio at six to listen to the news.

Weekends also meant freedom from the tyranny of time, such as his mother not yelling up the stairs at seven in the morning for him to get up to bring a bucket of coal from the cellar.

Once in a while, weekends involved a trip to Philadelphia by the way of the Reading Railway.

The first trip he remembered had been when he was five years old. Before the train arrived at Robinsville, he'd felt the slightest trembling of the platform under his feet. Then it bellowed into sight out of a tunnel that gaped beyond the curving of the tracks around a bend of the Schuylkill River. Belching a cloud of black from the smokestack at the front and gushing plumes of steam on both sides, it drew near, getting louder and louder, causing him to shrink back from the edge of the platform, his back pressed hard and flat against the wall of the station.

As the train roared and clattered and hissed and puffed and screeched and slowed up to huff to a stop, he had clapped hands over his ears. But it had not helped. The noise came up through his feet and thundered to the top of his head.

By age six he had not only become accustomed to the noise, but looked forward to standing there on a Saturday morning with his parents, Jack, and three sisters, who eagerly anticipated the day of shopping in department stores on Market Street. Then, the "All ah-bawd!" clambering to obey the command, lest the train go without him. Grabbing a seat by the window and drawing a line in the black soot that coated the sill. To feel the slam and jerk of car against car as the train lurched forward. Then picking up of speed and the clackety-clackety-clack-clack of steel wheels over little gaps between the steel rails. The excitement of the bridge just before they reached Norristown, where lived Aunt Ida and Uncle Alex, who owned a bar there. Then, much too soon, arrival amidst clouds of hissing steam at the vast, echoing barn that was the Reading Terminal.

Finally, after a day of shopping and visiting Uncle Harry, he'd jump on the 4:30 bound for Pottsville and Shamokin. But homeward-bound on a train was never as wondrous as getting on one to begin a journey.

On weekend mornings not including a train ride to Philly, Paulie was permitted to loaf in bed as long as he wished. Then he was usually allowed to stay up later on Saturday when he went with the whole family to a movie at the Colonial, and also on Fridays to the Rialto with Kate.

But as he left school on this Friday afternoon and looked forward to seeing *Tarzan's Secret Treasure* and *Wild Bill Hickok Rides*, he had a sinking feeling in his belly, brought on by the realization that Kate was starting a new job on Monday. Now they probably would not be going to movies together until the war was over. And once Mike came home and Kate married him, maybe they'd never again go the Rialto together.

At supper he gloomily pondered a future of movies without Kate beside him, hating the Nazis and Japs who had brought this about by starting a war. He stared vacantly into his soup bowl at the globules of melted butter floating on the milk and clustered around a half-submerged oyster, last of three, only to have Kate startle him with, "Hey, little brother, what's got you looking so down in the dumps?"

Wondering if she could read his mind, he blurted, "Nothin'."

Looking alarmed, his father demanded, "Is there a problem at school, Paulie?"

"Everything at school's fine."

With a smirk, Arlene looked up from her stew to interject in a singsong voice, "I heard that he's got a big crush on a girl in eighth grade by the name of Elaine Rose."

"Whoever told you that," Paulie said, turning red-faced as he fished for the last oyster with a spoon, "is a damn liar."

With a look that could very well doom a night at the Rialto with Kate, Thomas Fallon blared, "Watch your tongue, boy."

Like cavalry riding to the rescue in a cowboys-and-Indians movie, Kate said, "Is that the Rose family whose two youngest boys ran off to Philadelphia to join the Marine Corps the day after Pearl Harbor?"

Frowning, Mrs. Fallon said, "And broke a mother's heart."

Her husband said, "They were old enough to have been drafted sooner or later."

Relieved that his concerns about improper language had been deftly deflected, Paulie consumed the last oyster and smiled in gratitude at his rescuer. "There are two good movies at the Rialto tonight, Kate. A Tarzan and a Wild Bill Hickok."

Arriving downtown with ample time before the show started, Kate followed her usual practice of giving him a dime to spend at Woolworth's toy counter while she dropped in at the Book Nook.

Entering breezily, she said, "Hello, Mrs. Bee. Have any good mystery novels come in this week?"

Greeting Kate with a cat-that-ate-the-canary-smile, Beatrice answered, "Parcel post had no new thrillers, but I'm happy to say that the milkman, Mr. Groover, provided the answer to the mystery of John Bohannon's whereabouts."

"Really? Where is he?"

"Atlantic City. John left a note for Mr. Groover in an empty bottle telling him to suspend deliveries because he's gone deep-sea fishing."

"I must say, Atlantic City's the last place I'd choose to go fishing in February."

"You're not a man."

"I'm so glad Mr. Groover cleared up that mystery."

"I assume you and your little brother are off to the movies. What's on the bill this evening?"

"Tarzan and Wild Bill Hickok, but not, as far as I know, together in the same movie. I'm not certain, but I may have already seen both pictures. Jungle movies and Westerns have a tendency to look alike. Of course, all that matters to Paulie is that there's plenty of action."

"The young lad is blessed in having such an understanding and patient sister."

"He's helped me cope with a lot of loneliness since Mike went away," Kate said, peeking through the window at Paulie as he paced the sidewalk and shot her impatient glances. "I had better not keep the brat waiting any longer."

"Enjoy the show, my dear."

16

THE OWNER OF both Robinsville's movie houses built the second at the start of the Depression and presented a double feature for a quarter as a cheaper alternative to one picture at the Colonial for the same price. Whether or not he intended it especially for an audience of kids, the Rialto had become just that. With an interior that was nothing like the opulence of the Colonial's gilded trimmings, glittery chandeliers, center and side aisles, velvet seats, a large two-tiered balcony, and a richly brocaded golden curtain that rose slowly to reveal the screen, the Rialto had a long sloping auditorium with uninterrupted rows. There was no balcony, and a plain gray curtain that parted and opened rather jerkily. At the Colonial, candy was sold at a counter in a large lobby by a girl in a royal blue outfit, while the Rialto offered two vending machines in a space more like a small vestibule. And if moviegoers entered the Colonial after the show had started, they were escorted to seats by usherettes carrying flashlights. Latecomers at the Rialto found themselves on their own.

Another difference between the theaters was evident when the lights went down. The Colonial's audience hushed. At the Rialto there was an explosion of applause and a nearly deafening roar of excited young voices. How much the noise subsided depended on the type of movie. While mysteries and scary films would be watched in relative silence, cowboy pictures—in this instance, Wild Bill Hickock—were accompanied by a steady drone of comments and the sounds of candy boxes being ripped open. This undertone of murmured excitement also greeted every appearance of former Olympic swimming champion Johnny Weismuller since his introduction as a jungle hero in *Tarzan the Ape Man* in 1932. Then, Paulie was two years old and Kate had gone to the Rialto with her sisters. For 1934's *Tarzan and His Mate*, which introduced pretty Maureen O'Sullivan as Jane, she had gone with Mike. Later, mocking the scene in which Jane and Tarzan exchanged names, Mike pounded a fist on his chest and then hers and grunted "Tarzan, Jane." When Weismuller and O'Sullivan returned in *Tarzan Escapes*, Mike was away in college and six-year-old Paulie became her companion for Friday movies at the Rialto. Three years later when Johnny Sheffield appeared as Boy in *Tarzan Finds a Son*, she thought he looked like Paulie, except for Boy's curly blond hair. But in subsequent years Paulie had grown taller.

As she sat beside him in the middle of the seventh row back from the screen, she expected he soon would prefer to go to the Rialto alone or with friends. And one day with a girlfriend. But for now, here he sat, chewing Good & Plenty candy, and cheering Wild Bill and Tarzan as they fought evil in their unique ways.

With curtains closed and lights back on, it was time for the next phase of the Friday night ritual—ice cream sundaes, but this time it was at the long marble-topped soda fountain of Feicht's drugstore. Entering at a few minutes past nine, she saw Scrappy MacFarland at the tobacco counter and tapped him on the shoulder. "Does your mother know you smoke?"

Turning, he grinned. "Does you mom know you're out late?"

"Been to the movies. I never miss a Tarzan picture."

Scrappy looked down at Paulie. "Who's your date?"

"I thought you'd met my brother," Kate said, hugging Paulie as his face turned pink with embarrassment. "I used to call him my little brother, but he's growing up so fast, pretty soon he'll be tall enough to call me his little sister. Are you taking a break from getting out the paper?"

"Much to *my surprise* and consternation, I discovered I'd run out of cigars."

"I see you smoke Phillies cigars," Kate said, "the same as my dad."

"At three for a quarter," he said, slipping two cigars into the breast pocket of his jacket, "how could I go wrong?"

"What will I be reading in the *Independence* tomorrow?"

"Nothing sensational," he said, removing the cellophane from the third cigar. "It's not every day that somebody sets a fire in an attempt to conceal a murder."

"So it was murder? Jonas didn't kill himself?"

"As a rule, people do not shoot themselves in the back of the head."

"I can't imagine why anyone would murder Jonas Longacre."

Scrappy stuck the cigar in the right corner of his mouth. "As Phil Baker says on 'Take It Or Leave It', that's the sixty-four-dollar question." He paused, lighting the cigar. "May I assume, since you worked at Gordon's, that you knew Longacre?"

"Since the seventh grade."

"The word about him is that he was always a trouble-maker."

"I think it was less a matter of him making trouble than it was trouble finding him."

Scrappy plucked the cigar from his lips. "Now that's a very interesting observation. It gives me an idea. Since you knew him so well, and since you claim to know your way around a newspaper, and now that you've got some time on your hands on account of the fire wiping out your job, how'd you like to write an article for the paper? Was Jonas a naturally bad boy? Or did he turn out that way because of circumstances?"

"Gosh, that's very flattering, but I'm not going to have any time on my hands. I've got a new job starting Monday."

"Whoa! That was fast! What's the job?"

Paulie blurted, "She's going to be a *welder*."

Kate smiled nervously. "That's right. At Manyon's. Just for the duration, of course. If it all works out."

"Why shouldn't it? Girls are taking on all sorts of jobs because of the manpower shortage. I've been thinking about assigning Dick Levitan to put together a series on the subject for Saturday editions. Hey! How'd you like to be interviewed?"

"Scrappy, I haven't even started the job."

"So much the better. Levitan can be right there beside you from day one on the job."

"I don't think Mr. Manyon would care for that."

"I've known Jerome Manyon since he started his business in a garage. Nothing pleases him more than seeing his company's name in print, especially if he doesn't have to pay for it. Kate, this could be a terrific story on the contribution women are making to the war effort. It might even be picked up by a wire service and distributed coast to coast. You could wind up becoming the most famous woman in the United States, with the possible exception of Mrs. Roosevelt and, maybe, Kate Smith."

17

ON SUNDAY MORNING as Kate, her parents, Arlene, and Paulie approached the Presbyterian church, Kate read the sign on the front lawn of the gray-stone building. Borrowing a ringing phrase from President Roosevelt's speech to Congress on the day after Pearl Harbor, white letters on a black background stated the theme of the Rev. Richard Hilldale's sermon:

DOING OUR PART TO GAIN
THE INEVITABLE TRIUMPH

A young man, Hilldale was the fifth pastor of the church since Thomas Fallon had switched from the Episcopalian church across Gay Street when he was twenty-one years old because the Presbyterians had a baseball team and the Episcopalians did not.

The biblical text the Reverend Hilldale chose as inspiration for his sermon proved to be Old Testament. A verse from Genesis, it quoted Moses following the drowning of Pharaoh's army after the Red Sea swallowed it.

"Genesis, fifteen-seven," intoned Hilldale. " 'Thou sendest forth thy wrath which consumed them as stubble.' And so it shall be in this war, for as the Holy Bible states in Genesis, fifteen-three, 'The Lord is a man of war.' But this does not mean there will be a swift victory over our enemies. The day will come in which we rejoice in the defeat of God's and our foes, for it is true, as President Roosevelt declared, 'We shall gain the inevitable triumph.' But before we fulfill that pledge, we shall have to endure temporary defeats. Is God going to suddenly sweep down from Heaven to rescue our valiant soldiers on Bataan as He did at the Red Sea? No. But He will not forget their valor and their sacrifice, for they exhibit these virtues in His name. And he *will* remember them by rewarding their nation a victory that is certain as tomorrow's dawn."

This triumph, he declared, would be earned by heroes like the defenders of Wake Island. There, he reminded the congregation, four-hundred U.S. Marines and a thousand civilians had held off a Japanese invasion for sixteen days before being overwhelmed.

And the day before at Pearl Harbor, gallant Captain Colin Kelly piloted his B-17 over the Japanese battleship *Haruna* and sank it. According to the War Department, after his plane was hit, he ordered his crew to bail out while he stayed at the controls to sink the ship by crash-diving the bomber into its funnels.

"There will be many more such heroes before the

war's end," Hilldale said, "but not all of them will achieve that status in the heat of the battlefield."

Looking around the church, Kate noted how many young men were not present.

"I speak of the heroes here at home," Hilldale continued, "the people of all the Robinsvilles of the nation, who will fight for victory in countless ways: not hoarding, walking instead of taking the car, buying war bonds, turning out unnecessary lamps, and all the other things we are being asked to do, not because we might receive a medal, but simply because they are right. So, you see, we have all been called to serve, each of us in his and her own way, as our God and our nation require."

With a chill running down her back, Kate wondered if it were possible that God had decreed a fire to take away her job so she could fill a more purposeful one as a welder. But as quickly as the thought entered her mind, she rejected it. To believe so, she would also have to believe that God had looked the other way as the purpose of Mr. Gordon's entire life went up in flames.

Presently, inspired by the sermon's theme of a heavenly ordained victory in the war, the congregation rose to conclude the hour by spiritedly singing "Onward, Christian Soldiers."

Late Sunday night, Scrappy MacFarland listened to music of a different kind as he felt the rumble and vibrations of the press rolling out the *Independence* for Monday, February 23, 1942. Leaning back in a large tiltable chair, he lit his fifth cigar of the day and declared to the man opposite him, "Listen to that! The music of the night."

Slouching in a wooden armchair with his chin resting on his hand, Dick Levitan said, "I don't hear any music."

Scrappy plucked the cigar from his mouth. "A few years ago there was a movie called *Dracula*. There was a scene where Bela Lugosi, as the count, is standing on a stairway while wolves are howling in the distance. He says, 'Listen to them. The children of the night. What music they make.' That's the way I feel when I hear a press printing the day's news."

Making a sour face, Levitan dug a pack of Chesterfields from his shirt pocket. "There's not a hell of a lot of news coming off the press tonight. There never is in the Monday edition. I hate weekends. Nothing happens."

Scrappy folded meaty hands on his large belly and puffed a column of smoke. "The Japs bombed Pearl Harbor on a Sunday. The Edinger girl was found on Saturday. The Gordon factory burned down on a Saturday night. Jonas Longacre was found dead on Sunday."

"Yeah, but nothing's happened to advance the story since, and nothing will until our intrepid police chief officially says it's a murder case."

"What's preventing him?"

"The state police coroner has been asked to determine for sure that Longacre didn't blow his own brains out."

"Of course he didn't. I saw the bullet hole. It was in the middle of the back of the head."

"Ed Polansky thinks it might have been an exit wound."

Scrappy grunted. "Nuts. Where does he put the entry wound?"

"He thinks it could've been through the eye," Levitan said, making his right hand a pistol with the forefinger as a barrel pointing to his right eye. "Nobody shoots himself through an eye. *Between* the eyes, yes." He moved his hand and placed the finger to his right temple. "But usually it's here. Or in the mouth." The hand became a fist and banged the semicircular table. "But in the back of the head? In two words, IM POSSIBLE. For Jonas to plug himself in the back of his noggin, he would have had to be a carnival-sideshow contortionist."

18

WHILE THE CONVERSATION unfolded in the city room of the *Independence*, Kate Fallon was finding sleep difficult. Tossing and turning, she felt the kind of anxiety she had experienced on the night before Mr. Bohannon was to test her knowledge of history, never her strongest subject. It was the same nervousness which had gripped her before her first date with Mike.

Now she worried not only about him, but about how he might feel when he received the letter she had lain awake composing in her mind, telling him she had taken the welding job, and worrying what he might say when he wrote back.

Finally having dropped off around four, she was awakened at six o'clock by the rattling of bottles as Mr. Groover delivered milk to the neighborhood.

Going back to sleep was out of the question because

she had to be up at seven in order to report to Mr. Manyon at eight.

Getting out of bed, she sat at her dressing table, opened her diary to the date, picked up a fountain pen Mike had given her one Christmas, and wrote with slightly trembling hand, "Today I start my new job. I hope I am doing the right thing. I *pray* Mike will not be upset about it."

Wearing a blue V-neck, long-sleeve sweater, a white blouse with narrow collar, red-and-green-plaid slacks, blue socks, flat black shoes, and a brown hair net, she went downstairs and found the kitchen floor dotted with heaps of clothing. Pouring a bucket of hot water into the washing machine, as she had been doing every Monday morning as long as Kate could remember, her mother greeted her. "Morning, Kate. Do I have everything of yours?"

"Yes, I think so," Kate said, giving her a feathery kiss on the forehead and looking at Paulie alone at the table, eating a bowl of corn flakes. "Has Arlene gone to school already?"

"Monday is her early day. She has band practice, just as you used to."

Remembering futile efforts to master the mysteries of the clarinet, Kate sat opposite Paulie. With a heaping spoonful of soggy flakes dripping milk midway between his bowl and mouth, he studied her intently. He demanded, "Are you wearing that thing to work?"

Kate poured half a bowl of the cereal. "What do you mean?"

Chewing, he pointed the spoon at her. "That goofy-looking thing you've got around your hair."

Kate patted the net. "Of course I'm wearing this to work. That's why I bought it. I got two of them, in fact."

"Welders wear those things?"

"*Women* welders do," she said, adding milk to her bowl. "It's a safety requirement. I'll also be wearing a pair of coveralls."

Paulie giggled. "Gee-*zuz*, I'd really love to see that!"

Taking a half step away from the stove. Mrs. Fallon smacked his shoulder. "Watch your mouth, boy."

Kate said, "Since you and I will now be leaving at the same time every morning, Paulie, you can walk me to the bus stop. You can talk to me and keep me from being nervous."

"What's to be nervous about?"

"Starting something new is always a scary time. I feel as jumpy as I did on my first day of school. But then I didn't have to worry about getting fired."

"Come on," Paulie said with a chuckle, "you won't be fired."

"Of course you won't," said Mrs. Fallon. "I don't know what they do about lunch at that factory, so I packed you a bag lunch of a couple of baloney and cheese sandwiches and a banana."

A few streets away as Beatrice Bradshaw opened her kitchen door in response to knocks with the rhythm of "Shave and a haircut, two bits," she noticed a light had been left on all night on the back porch of Eleanor Murray's house. For no other reason than to have something to say, she mentioned it as the milkman handed her the two quarts that would last her the entire week.

"No need to fret about that light," declared Mr. Groover. "The police have given her special permission."

"Really? When did they do that?"

"Last Monday night, after she reported a suspicious man in her backyard."

Beatrice laughed. "Another one? Was a man really there?"

"If so, he was gone by the time the police came. Anyway, she told me that the officers told her they would fix it with somebody in Washington so she could leave the light on."

Later, as Don McNeill and *The Breakfast Club* were going off the air and Mary Edinger sat at her table sipping coffee, Beatrice concluded her account of the light with, "In my opinion, the only men Eleanor Murray sees are imaginary."

"That's what I said to her when she told me about seeing the man. I said, 'Ellie, you always see things that ain't there.' But she insisted she saw a man cutting through her backyard in the direction of Mr. Bohannon's house." Glancing at the clock above Beatrice's stove, she said, "I guess Kate Fallon isn't joining us this morning."

"Oh dear, didn't I tell you? Kate took my advice. She saw Mr. Manyon and got herself one of those welding jobs. She starts this morning. I offered to drive her to the factory, but she said she'd better begin getting accustomed to taking the bus to work."

Mary sighed. "We're all going to have to get used to things we wouldn't have given one moment of thought to before the war."

Beatrice looked out the window at slate gray skies. "I think we may be in for some snow. Is your pantry well stocked, Mary? If not, I can drop you at the A&P store on my way downtown. Or I can stop there coming home and pick up anything you might need."

"Thanks, but I'm fine," said Mary, correctly reading Beatrice's signal that it was time for her to go home.

"If you think of anything, ring me at the store," Beatrice said, as Mary crossed a narrow swath of lawn between their houses, "I'll be there till five o clock."

Crossing her front lawn toward her Buick, she saw the mailman going up the steps of the John Bohannon's front porch. "Good morning, Mr. Granick." she said, approaching him. "Anything for me?"

A short, slight man, he always appeared too frail to carry the bulging brown-leather bag that seemed permanently attached to his left hip. He tipped a blue cap. "Nothing this morning. If you're expecting something, perhaps I'll have it this afternoon."

"No, nothing's expected," she said, noting that the mailbox next to Bohannon's door was crammed with letters. "I'm afraid I'm not as popular as my neighbor."

Granick frowned at the letter box. "I wish he'd told me he was going to be away."

"It came as a surprise to me, as well. He's on an expedition to Atlantic City. Deep-sea fishing."

"If this box gets any fuller, I'll have to bundle the mail up and hold it for him at the post office." Looking down at an accumulation of newspapers, he continued, "He should've informed the paperboy, too. It's not a good idea to let things pile up like this. It might attract burglars. I'm not sure I'll be able to jam this morning's mail into that little box."

"Would it be all right if I held it for him?"

"Well, it's not customary under regulations," Granick said, staring at the stuffed box, "without the addressee's permission."

"I take your point, and it's a reasonable policy, but leaving Mr. Bohannon's mail with me would spare you all the trouble of having to carry it back to the post office."

Granick drummed fingers on his mail pouch. "Any idea when he'll be coming back?"

"As I said, I didn't even know he was going away. He could return today, or not for a week. He *is* retired, and he certainly does enjoy fishing."

Granick shifted the pouch's carrying strap higher on his narrow shoulder. "One of the few things that bum President Herbert Hoover said when he was in office was that the amount of time a man spends fishing is added by God to his lifetime. I'm an angler myself. Trout, when it's the season." He paused, gazing at the box and the four letters in his hand. "I guess it don't make a lot of sense for me to lug all that mail downtown, only to have Mr. Bohannon call down to the post office for it to be delivered again. Go ahead and take it. I'll write a note and stick it in the box telling him you have the mail. Maybe you should take the newspapers away, too." With a little cackling laugh, he added, "At least Mr. Bohannon thought to tell the milkman to cut off his deliveries, otherwise this porch might be covered with bottles of soured milk and cream."

"Given the cold spell we've been having," Beatrice said, pulling the mail from the box, "it's more likely to have frozen."

The mailman peered at the glowering clouds. "It looks

like we may be in for some snow. Driving home tonight you might need tire chains on you car."

"If we have that much snow," Beatrice said, going down the porch steps, "I'll leave my old jalopy parked downtown and take the bus home."

19

SNOWFLAKES MELTED ON the windows of a hallway connecting the Manyon Precision Metals Company's office building with the adjoining factory. Mr Manyon stood, speaking to Kate. "The fella who'll be training you is Ivo Bogdanovich. But to everybody in the plant he's Plug. That's not because he's always got a plug of chewing tobacco stuffed in his cheek, which he does. He got the nickname because he's squat and solid like a fireplug."

They stopped in front of a door on which had been tacked a paper sign with penciled lettering: WOMEN ONLY.

"So far you're the only one," Manyon said. "It's really a men's room, but everyone's been told of the change, so you don't have to worry about anyone walking in on you. You can use it to change into your overalls before and after your shift in case you decide to leave them here instead of taking them home. I'm sorry it's not closer to where you'll be working. It's the best I could come up with. I'll wait while you change, and then I'll turn you over to Plug."

Leaving her lunch bag and her purse, she came out of the converted men's room in slightly baggy gray overalls and found Manyon regarding her with a worried expression.

"That won't do," he said. "I'll see if I can find something closer to your size."

"There's no need. One thing I learned at school, in addition to typing is sewing. I'll take these and the other pair home tonight and do a little nipping and tucking."

"I wish all my problems could be solved that easily. And now that you're properly dressed, I'll turn you over to Plug. He may look intimidating and sound a little like Edward G. Robinson in *Little Caesar*, but he's really a sweetheart."

"I hope for his sake that he's got the patience of Job. He's going to need it."

As they walked to the door of the factory, he said, "You're probably feeling a trifle nervous, I imagine."

"Nervous? I'm *petrified*."

"No need to be. There's no better man at teaching the tricks of the welder's trade than Plug," he said.

As he opened the door, she entered a long, low-ceilinged, cavernous-looking space of noise, flying sparks, smoke, and the smell of something burning. She wondered if somehow she had been led through one of the gates of Hell itself. Passing men wearing metal masks and wielding flame-spitting metal wands she followed Manyon deeper into the welding shop.

With falling snow visible through windows that appeared to never have been washed, she found Ivo "Plug" Bogdanovich just as Manyon had described him physically.

Speaking in the twangy, nasal tone of a movie gangster but with a charming foreign accent, he provided data so rapidly that all the welding terms created a blizzard in her head.

Cold welding uses high pressure at room temperature.

Forge welding also uses pressure, only lower, and hammering with heat added.

The metal is melted at the points that we want joined with what is called filler to help bond the pieces.

One kind of hot welding is called the Thompson process. It uses electric current to make heat.

"We'll start you off by practicing with bits of scrap," he said, "and then take it from there."

Three hours and a growing pile of welded metal chunks later, he signaled her to stop. "You pick it up fast," he said as she lifted her mask. "You'll do good. But now you break to eat, and I will introduce you to the men you'll be working with."

Feeling the sudden clutching of anxiety in her stomach, stronger even than her hunger, she blurted a lie. "Lunch! I'm afraid I left mine at home on the kitchen table."

"No matter. You can share mine. I always bring two hoagies."

Anxiety became panic. "Oh, Plug, I couldn't do that."

"Why not? You can pay me back for the hoagy on payday."

"That's very nice of you, but—"

Plug smiled slyly. "I think you're nervous and afraid the men might not be nice to you. You think they'll be crude. Maybe make jokes?"

Kate removed the mask. "They might need a little more time to get used to a woman being around."

"It don't matter what they think. Mr. Manyon hired you, and that's that. And they don't run this shop. I run it. The sooner they get used to you being around, the better. And if anybody in the shop thinks he can try giving you a hard time, well, he's got another think coming, because I happen to know that Mr. Manyon's already hired two more women starting next week."

When the whistle sounded again at four o'clock, Kate felt tapping on her shoulder. Turning off the acetylene torch and tilting back her mask, she found Mr. Manyon smiling broadly.

Looking at the stack of welded chunks of metal, he said, "I never thought I'd be saying this to a woman, but young lady, you have obviously got a natural ability for welding. Plug recommends I cut your time as an apprentice to one week. All in all, I would say you've made a good impression on the men. So, after putting in a first day's work, how do you feel about it?"

Kate wiped her brow with the back of a hand and let out a gust of breath. "I can't wait to get home and soak in a bubble bath for a few hours."

Manyon laughed. "Enjoy your bath. Get a good night's sleep. I'll see you in the morning."

At six o'clock, barely able to restrain her excitement, Beatrice Bradshaw looked at her kitchen clock to be certain she would not disturb Kate's supper and picked up the telephone.

In the formal manner Kate taught him, Paulie answered, "This is the Fallon residence."

"It's Mrs. Bradshaw, Paulie. Is Kate at home?"

"Just a moment, please."

"Thank you."

Paulie shouted, "Hey, Kate. Telephone for you. It's the lady from the bookstore."

A moment later, Kate offered a cheerful, "Hi, Mrs. Bee."

"I hope I'm not interrupting anything."

"I was about to do a little sewing. The coveralls I wear at work need taking in."

"How did your first day on the job go?"

"Mr. Manyon said I have a natural talent for welding. And how was your day?"

"Mondays at the store are always slow. But I do have something exciting to tell you. As I always do when Mr. Bohannon is away, I emptied his mailbox so that it wouldn't overflow. I found a letter from a Miss Elvira Eveland. She's an editor at a New York book publishing firm. Evidently, he wrote to her concerning his book. I had no idea he'd finished it."

"Do you suppose her letter is an offer to publish? Wouldn't that be a thrill? And what an honor for Robinsville to have its own resident author!"

"Don't get too excited, my dear. The letter could contain a rejection slip."

"It's a pity you don't know where Mr. Bohannon is staying on his fishing trip. If you knew, you could call him and tell him about the letter."

"Well, I suppose we'll just have to wait until he gets

back. I'm glad it's going well for you in your new job. I'll let you get back to your sewing. I have a few things to get out of the way before President Roosevelt comes on the radio."

"He's speaking tonight?"

"Yes, at eight o'clock."

Speaking of the thousands of American troops engaged in combat in the Pacific, President Roosevelt confidently declared, "Soon, we and not our enemies will have the offensive."

He continued, "The American Eagle is neither an ostrich nor a turtle. We will continue increasingly the policy of carrying the war to the enemy in distant lands, distant waters. We have most certainly suffered losses—from Hitler's U-boats in the Atlantic as well as from the Japanese in the Pacific—and we shall suffer more of them before the turn of the tide."

With the familiar voice that always sounded to Kate like a mixture of a father talking common sense to his children and a preacher sermonizing that faith will always triumph, Roosevelt brimmed with optimism. "Soon, *we* and not our enemies, will have the offensive," he declared, "*we*, not they, will win the final battles; and *we*, not they, will make the final peace."

Proud and inspired, yet at the same time longing for Mike, Kate turned off the radio and put her recording of "I'll Be Seeing You" on the phonograph. Sinatra evoked melancholy memories of Mike in all their old familiar places, of doing things bright and gay with him, and of lovely summer days spent together before the war ruined everything.

Part 4

Old Familiar Places

20

FOUR DAYS AFTER Roosevelt's address, on the first Friday night since his sister had become a welder, Paulie studied Kate wistfully across the supper table and feared that if he asked her to go to the movies she would claim to be too tired. Or perhaps she'd say she had other things to do, such as washing her hair or catching up on reading since she had been so busy all week she'd been unable to even pick up a book. But as he stared at crumbled saltine crackers floating in oyster stews, trying to sink them with a spoon as if it was a torpedo plane attacking U-boats, she startled him by asking, "What's playing at the Rialto tonight, Paulie?"

With spirits rising hopefully he exclaimed excitedly, "It's *Charlie Chan in Rio* and *Mad Doctor of Market Street*."

"Ooo, that sounds awfully scary. You might get nightmares. Maybe we should go to the Colonial. What's playing there?"

As Paulie replied with a shrug, Arlene answered. "It's *A Yank on the Burma Road*. It's a war picture with Laraine Day."

Thomas Fallon spoke up. "I figured in celebration of your first week on your job, and to give your mother a relief from having to cook, we'd all have supper downtown tomorrow and then go see that show together. I like Laraine Day."

Kate winked at Paulie. "Then the Rialto it is."

Although she managed to stay awake until Mr. Chan solved a murky mystery involving hypnotism induced by cigarettes and black coffee, she fell asleep halfway through a tame thriller about an insane scientist using Pacific island natives for his strange experiments.

An hour later at Buster's as Paulie noisily sipped the last drops of a chocolate milk shake through a straw, she yawned, and said, "I'm going to borrow a leaf from your book and stay in bed until two in the afternoon."

"Not me," Paulie said, licking the straw. "I'll be getting up early to go skating with Donny Hartzel at Fulmer's Pond."

"Are you sure it's thick enough to skate on?"

"Donny says it's been froze solid for a week."

"Fro-ZEN solid. I don't want to hear that a kid fell through the thin ice and drowned and then be told it was you."

Paulie looked at her incredulously. "The spot where we skate is only three feet deep."

Kate placed a half dollar on the counter to cover the

milk shakes and a ten-cent tip. "A person can drown in a bathtub."

"Sure," Paulie said, cackling and bounding off the stool, "if somebody's holding his head under the water."

Kate's intention to sleep late was foiled at six o'clock with the relentless barking of the Hartzels' dog. She gazed at the faint glimmer of the dawn light on the bedroom ceiling and marveled that so tiny a terrier could produce such a persistent nerve-grating racket. As other dogs in the neighborhood responded to the sound, forming a raucus chorus, she recognized the unlikelihood of ever getting back to sleep.

Out of bed, she wondered as she put on a thick sweater and slacks if Mike was also awake. Could he have been rudely jolted from sleep by a real-life version of the boogie woogie bugle boy?

Combing her hair and hoping Mike was also thinking of her at that moment, she heard the familiar squeak of brakes from the boxlike, white-and-green Trainer's Dairy delivery truck driven by Mr. Groover. This was followed by the rattling of bottles as he carried a rectangular metal basket to the porch and left four quarts of milk then picked up the empties Mrs. Fallon never failed to set out the night before.

Passing Kate's open door on her way downstairs to the kitchen, mindful that Paulie and Arlene were still sleeping, Mrs. Fallon said quietly, "I see you're already up, Kate. I thought you were going to sleep late today."

Kate shrugged. "The Hartzel's dog had other ideas."

"One of these days somebody's going to shoot that animal," said Mrs. Fallon, her voice fading as she went down the stairs, "and it will be good riddance to bad rubbish."

Moments later, Kate heard the scraping of a small shovel as her mother scooped coal from a scuttle into the kitchen stove. Next she would be carrying a tall white coffeepot to the sink, adding cold water from the spigot, and heaping tablespoons of Chase and Sanborn into a little metal basket.

"One per cup, and one for the pot," her mother had taught her long ago. Chase and Sanborn, she insisted, because it was the sponsor of the Edgar Bergen and Charlie McCarthy program, a radio show she tried never to miss. With the coffeepot on the stove, the milk would be brought in, along with the *Independence*, providing the paperboy who delivered it on Saturdays did not oversleep.

During the night, as he had contemplated the front page layout for the last day of February, Scrappy Mac-Farland had been torn between giving the main headline to a war despatch from the Pacific and Dick Levitan's story on the school board narrowing its search for William Street's replacement.

Chewing a soggy black stump of a Philly, he glared at Levitan across his desk. "How the hell long does it take to hire a principal for a junior high school?"

"Well, it's not my job to defend the board," Levitan said, shifting nervously in his chair, "but it's not as if Street up and quit at the end of the term."

"Quit my foot! The guy was canned. That's the real story in all this, Richard."

"We sure as hell aren't going to get the inside scoop

from anybody on the board, and the central figure in this little drama has clammed up."

At that moment the phone rang, and Scrappy answered it with customary gruffness. "*Independence*, MacFarland." But the tone of impatience immediately turned to excitement. "What's that make, seven? Okay, six. Thanks, Jim. Dick's on his way."

As Scrappy hung up, Levitan asked, "On my way where?"

"Feicht's drugstore. That was Jim Kerner. He says he almost nabbed the guys who've been knocking over stores."

Rising, Levitan said, "Guys?"

"Two of 'em, apparently. But they lammed before Kerner could grab them, or see them well enough to identify them. I'll hold the front page till I hear from you. And while you're at it, see if you can find out the latest dope from the *gendarmes* on the search for whoever put that slug in Jonas Longacre's booze-soaked noggin six nights ago."

Levitan dug a pack of Chesterfields from his shirt pocket. "I could write that story this minute, and your headline would be 'Police Department Still Stumped.'"

"That's not a bad idea, Richard. When you're done with the attempted burglary, give me a couple of paragraphs. Maybe it'll goose the coppers into action. As for now, even with the try at breaking into Feicht's, it looks like the main headline will be the war news. I just hope one day soon it will be better. I'm longing to see the word VICTORY in large type across the front page."

Levitan lit the Lucky. "FDR says you soon will."

As his best reporter walked away from the desk,

Scrappy gave a grunt and lit another cigar. "Would you say different on radio coast to coast and broadcast to the American people if you were sitting in the White House?"

Raising a hand with two fingers raised in a Churchillian V-for-victory gesture, Levitan replied, "The American people can thank their lucky stars I'm not."

An hour later, precisely on schedule, the press in the basement rumbled to life so that a small army of sleepy-eyed kids with *Independence* pouches hanging from the handlebars of bicycles could fling rolled-up copies of the newspaper onto front porches. Then, at their leisure, subscribers would read of disheartening war news, an attempted burglary, and no progress in the Longacre or Edinger murders. Or that of Sara Griffith.

21

WHEN KATE FALLON stepped onto the front porch at a quarter past six, milk bottles left by Mr. Groover had not been standing in the cold long enough for the cream to freeze and pop up the paper bottle caps. Picking up the four quarts and the newspaper, she decided it was not the sort of day for anyone to be outdoors for any length of time. It was definitely unsuitable for hiking the three miles to Fulmer's Pond and spending hours ice-skating.

Entering a kitchen already nicely warmed by the coals in the ungainly iron stove, she declared, "It's brutally cold out this morning. I don't think it's such a good idea for Paulie to go ice-skating."

Mrs. Fallon spoke without looking up from her cooking. "Who told you he's going ice-skating?"

"He did, last night."

"Well, he's got another think coming. Your father expects him to help out with fixing one side of the coal bin. A couple of the boards need shoring up, and he wants to get it done before we get the next delivery on Monday. So don't you worry your pretty head about Paulie going ice-skating. He'll be spending most of the day snug and warm in the cellar."

Putting the milk into the Frigidaire, Kate said, "Paulie's going to be upset when he finds out. He'll be pouting all day."

As two eggs and three slices of bacon went onto a plate for Kate, Mrs. Fallon said, "He can pout all he wants. The coal bin needs fixing, so that's that. What are your plans for today?"

"I was going to go downtown and drop in at the Book Nook to see what's new. But it is awfully cold. On the other hand, I've always found it wise not to be anywhere in the vicinity when my spoiled brat of a little brother goes on the warpath."

"And whose fault is it that Paulie's spoiled? Yours."

"*Mine?*"

"At least since Mike went into the army."

Kate thought a moment, picked up a strip of crisp bacon, and nodded emphatically. "Guilty as charged. But isn't that as it's supposed to be between the oldest and youngest in a family?"

"You spend too much on him. You're always giving him nickels and dimes, taking him to movies, buying sundaes."

"That's because he keeps me from feeling . . . well, when I take Paulie to see a movie, or we're having sundaes at Buster's, or milk shakes at Feicht's, I don't feel quite so—"

"Quite so lonely?"

Kate nodded. "It's no criticism of you and Dad and Arlene, but in the hours I spend at the movies with Paulie it's as though there's no war. I feel the same when I'm with Mrs. Bee down at the Book Nook. Maybe it's because she is so much older than I and Paulie's so much younger, but when I'm with them it's as if the world has not gone completely insane."

Turning to the morning paper, she nibbled bacon while glancing at the depressing main headline:

ALLIES IN JAVA SEA BATTLE WITH JAPS;
    BATAAN DEFENDERS STILL HANG ON BRAVELY.

Next, her eye settled on:

EDINGER AND LONGACRE MURDERS: POLICE
    STILL STUMPED

Beside this was the headline:

    DOWNTOWN BURGLARY FOILED,
        TWO MEN BARELY ESCAPE CAPTURE.

Reading the story, she gasped, "My gosh, Jim Kerner almost caught somebody trying to get into Feicht's drugstore."

Banging noises upstairs caused her to look at the ceiling. "It appears the spoiled brat is getting up. I think it's time to get out of the direct line of fire."

Mrs. Fallon demanded, "And where are you going this early?"

"I'll be at Mrs. Bee's house for a cup of coffee and maybe one of her scones. Then I might go along with her to the store and see if there are any new mysteries."

"You and your murder stories!"

As clomping footsteps on the stairs signaled the imminent arrival of an ill-fated brother, Kate gobbled the last strip of bacon.

His shoulder draped with ice skates linked by long tied laces as Kate went out the door, Paulie looked quizzically at his mother, and asked, "Where's she going already?"

"Never you mind about Kate," answered Mrs. Fallon. "Sit down and eat your breakfast. And you can put away the skates. Your dad has a job for you that's going to take all day."

Buttoning her overcoat and looping a yellow scarf over her head to cover her ears, Kate listened sympathetically to Paulie's long groan of anguish.

Walking briskly, she soon questioned the wisdom of being outside on a brutally cold morning. While she found few Robinsville residents braving the weather, some had ventured as far as their automobiles, only to find their engines reluctant to start. On many porches she passed, the *Independence* lay where it landed and the paper caps of milk bottles rested atop upraised cylinders of frozen cream. Columns of smoke rose almost straight from the chimneys of houses with frosty windows.

Turning a corner and passing John Bohannon's house,

she wondered if he had come back from his fishing trip. Quickening her pace toward Mrs. Bee's house, she eagerly anticipated cozy warmth, freshly baked scones, and hot coffee in the snug kitchen.

22

Seated in Beatrice's kitchen, Kate declared, "That collie of Mrs. Murray's is much too large for such a tiny, elderly woman. And not only that, a woman of her advanced age should not be out in these freezing temperatures. And for her to drag that poor dog along borders on animal cruelty."

"I'm sure both dog and Eleanor will survive, Kate," Beatrice said as she placed delicate china coffee cups and saucers with a matching plate piled with scones on the table. "I only hope that if I live to be Eleanor's age I'll be *able* to walk."

A loud knocking caused her to turn to the door. "Who in the world can that be?" Opening the door, she found Eleanor Murray.

Breathless and ashen-faced, the woman blurted, "Oh Beatrice, thank God you're here. You're just the person to make the phone call. If I do it, the police will think I've been seeing things again and take their time coming out to investigate."

"Best get out of the cold, my dear," said Beatrice, drawing her into the kitchen. "Please try to be calm so you can tell Kate and me what you've seen that needs investigation."

"I was walking the dog and he got away from me. He ran into Mr. Bohannon's backyard. When I finally caught up with him he was on the back stoop. He was sniffing around the kitchen door, but when I went up the steps to get him, he was squatted on his haunches and howling. That's when I smelled a bad odor. At first I thought maybe an animal had crawled beneath the porch and died. But the smell seemed to be coming from inside the house, so I peeked in the kitchen door window and that's when I saw Mr. Bohannon lying dead on the floor."

Kate gasped. "Dead? Are you sure?"

"Oh yes, because of the smell! I nearly fainted from it. And the look of him, the face all swelled up. The eyes wide-open and staring back at me. The mouth was gaping horribly. If you don't believe me, come and see for yourself."

A few minutes later Thomas Detwiler rose from the breakfast table in his robe and pajamas when his wife called out that he had a phone call. With the *Independence* folded twice and propped against a sugar bowl, he glowered at the word *stumped* in the headline on the Longacre murder. Consequently, he greeted Beatrice with a grumpy "Hullo."

"Sorry to disturb you at home, Tom."

"It's quite all right," he lied, looking forlornly at his breakfast, expecting that by the time Beatrice got off the phone it would be cold. "I trust nothing's amiss at your store?"

"I'm calling you from my home."

"What's the trouble there?"

"I'm afraid I have a death to report."

"Whose?"

"My next-door neighbor John Bohannon. He's lying dead on his kitchen floor. The circumstances appear quite mysterious."

"*Mysterious*? In what way?"

"He's supposed to be at the Jersey shore, deep-sea fishing."

"Well, I expect there's a perfectly logical explanation for what happened. I hope you didn't touch anything in the house."

"Of course not," she said sharply. "I saw the body through a window. I knew better than to enter a possible crime scene."

"Let's not go jumping to any conclusions, Beatrice. You know how quick rumors get started in this town. I'll get a pair of my men out there right away, and I'll put in a call to Ed Polansky."

Probationary Officer Mickey Ludlum answered the phone at police headquarters with a quarter of an hour to go before the end of a mercifully quiet overnight shift. Todd Doebling was seated with his feet crossed on his desk, glancing anxiously at a wall clock and hoping nothing had happened to keep him from going home on time. But with a sinking heart, he heard Ludlum say, "Good morning, Chief. Brookview Avenue. We'll meet you there."

As Ludlum hung up, Doebling groaned. "Oh please tell me it's not old lady Murray seeing another prowler."

Ludlum grinned. "This time it's a dead body."

Buttoning his uniform, Doebling yawned. "The sooner we get out to Brookview Avenue, the sooner the chief lets you and me call it a day. I need my rest. Tonight I'm off duty, and I've got a date who looks better in a sweater than Lana Turner."

In nearly twenty years as a mortician, Ed Polansky had come to expect early telephone calls informing him of a corpse to be collected, although the call usually did not come from the chief of police. The last report of a death under possibly suspicious circumstances had been the Edinger murder.

After telephoning two burly young part-time assistants who carried bodies for him, he made another phone call.

23

SCRAPPY MACFARLAND PARKED his Chevy behind Polansky's Cadillac hearse and emerged to find the coroner, Chief Detwiler, Officers Doebling and Ludlum, and three women on the sidewalk in front of the address Polansky had whispered over the phone.

As he gave a nod of greeting toward Beatrice Bradshaw, Kate Fallon, and Eleanor Murray, Scrappy was met by a red-faced chief of police. "All right, MacFarland, why the hell are you here?"

Scrappy grinned. "And a good morning to you, also, Chief."

Standing close, Detwiler demanded, "Who tipped you off?"

Scrappy glanced at Polansky and, tapping a finger to his nose, replied, "Let's just say that I caught the smell of death in the air."

Detwiler stepped back. "Well, keep that overgrown schnoz of yours at a distance until I have something to say. *If* I have something to say." Turning to Polansky, he muttered, "Come on, Ed. The body's in the kitchen."

Standing in the doorway, Polansky saw the corpse lying facedown in the middle of the kitchen floor. A black cast-iron coal stove was to the right. Along the wall to the left was a sink with cabinets above and below. A closed door, he presumed, led to the cellar. The dining room was visible through an archway, with the parlor beyond at the front of the house. A small round table was overturned, and scattered around it were a broken coffee cup and saucer, slices of dry toast, a teaspoon, a bowl surrounded by spilled sugar, and a creamer whose contents had run out to form a long-since-congealed pool. Beside the body was a puddle of dried milk, spilled when two quart bottles fell to the floor and broke.

After Ed performed a cursory examination, kneeling beside the body, he looked up at Detwilwer and declared, "There appear to have been two crushing blows to the back of the head. Either was potentially fatal. I'll have to perform an autopsy to know for sure. But I can certainly confirm that you've got yourself another homicide."

"I see it happening like this," said the chief. "Bohannon was eating breakfast. Either he was interrupted and attacked with no warning, causing him to fall over and take the table with him. Or somebody was in here with him and they got into a dispute which turned into a struggle. That ended with Bohannon being hit on the head. But with what?"

Polansky rose. "The wounds suggest the object was curved."

Detwiler looked around the kitchen. "There's a coal shovel by the stove. Could it have been that?"

Polansky shook his head. "Not heavy enough."

The chief's eyes shifted up to a cast-iron skillet on top of the stove. "That frying pan maybe?"

"If that was the weapon," Polansky said, "I can't see why it was put back. In fact, I don't see anything in this kitchen that looks like the weapon."

Detwiler rubbed his jaw. "So whatever was used, the killer took it with him. How long do you suppose he's been dead?"

"Hard to say. The decomposition of the body appears to have been slowed by the cold wave we've been having the past couple of weeks. With no fire going in the stove, this room's as cold as an icebox. He could've died a week or more ago. I can't give you a better estimate of the time of death until I do an autopsy."

"Can you get to it right away?"

"I've got the hearse and two men waiting."

Staring at the body, Detwiler recalled the scornful tone of the newspaper article about the lack of progress in the Longacre murder and decided his only course was to tell Scrappy the truth.

Consequently, surrounded by the three women and a crowd of curious neighbors, he said, "It appears Mr. Bohannon was killed by an intruder, most likely by a stranger and perhaps an outsider passing through town. I hope the good people of Robinsville will understand that solving this case may take some time."

Jotting the quotation in a small notebook, Scrappy smiled and thought, *And a whole lot of luck.*

24

WITH KATE AND Eleanor Murray following her, Beatrice barged into her kitchen, and exclaimed in disgust, "He hopes the people of Robinsville will understand that solving this case may take some time. That's three murders committed in as many weeks. What kind of police force do we have in this town?"

"It doesn't surprise me a bit," said Murray, settling into a chair. "Instead of searching my yard when I reported a prowler, one of them told me that I if left my light on, prowlers would be frightened away. They thought I'd been imagining things. Well, I wasn't. I know there *was* a man in the yard. My dog barked at him. I *saw* him going in the direction of Mr. Bohannon's house. I'll bet you dollars to doughnuts that prowler killed him."

Kate asked, "What date was that, Miss Murray?"

She thought a moment. "It will be two weeks on Monday."

Kate nodded gravely and began pacing the kitchen. "And, Mrs. Bee, am I correct that it was the very next day that Mr. Groover found the note stating Mr. Bohannon had gone on a fishing trip?"

"That's right. John must have put up the note and come back into the house and surprised the intruder."

Leaning against a cupboard door with her arms folded, Kate said. "It's possible, of course. But if I were going away and I planned to leave a note, I'd do so on the way out."

Beatrice wagged finger at Kate. "Something is going on in that clever head of yours. What are you thinking?"

Kate shrugged. "Suppose the note was left by the killer."

"What a provocative idea?"

Mystified, Murray shook her head. "Why would he do that?"

"Because he was smart," Kate said. "He feared Mr. Bohannon's unexplained absence might concern someone enough that he or she would investigate. Posting the note bought the killer time to make his getaway."

Beatrice sighed. "I wish I *had* investigated. When I think of John lying dead all this time only a few feet away from my house I feel sick about not being suspicious."

Kate crossed the room and patted Beatrice's shoulder. "Just be glad the killer left the note, Mrs. Bee. It means Mr. Bohannon was *not* the victim of an intruding stranger."

Beatrice frowned. "I'm afraid I don't follow you."

"The killer left that note because he knew Mr. Bohannon well enough to appreciate he'd be missed right away," Kate said, again pacing the room and thinking aloud. "Who would care if he were to be missed? Surely not someone who was wandering through town and by chance entered Mr. Bohannon's house to burglarize it, only to get caught in the act. I think the person who crept through Miss Murray's backyard *was* going to Mr. Bohannon's house and ended up killing him."

Mrs. Murray looked at Kate incredulously. "I honestly don't know what's happening to this town. It used to be such a quiet and peaceful place. It was bad enough that all these burglaries are going on. Now we've had three more murders!"

"Three *more* murders?"

"Have you forgotten poor old Sara Griffith?"

"Of course not. But her murder was unlike those of Nancy and Jonas. Their deaths were premeditated. The police theory was that Sara was killed because she surprised someone who'd broken into her home."

"I've never believed that's what happened. I think she was marked for murder."

Beatrice blurted, "Nonsense. Who would want to kill Sara Griffith?"

"Perhaps we'll find out when Mr. Bohannon's book is published."

"How on earth do you know that his book deals with the Sara Griffith murder?"

"I don't *know for sure*, but when I ran into him at the post office a couple of weeks ago he told me that the package he was sending registered mail to a New York publisher was a book he'd written about an unsolved murder case in a small town. I assumed it was about the

Sara Griffith murder. And there was the argument he'd gotten into about it with the mailman, Mr. Groover and his son one morning as I was walking my dog. I clearly recall him telling them he had his own theory about who committed the murder. Now that he's dead, I suppose we're never going to know what he thought."

"You're wrong, Eleanor," said Beatrice. "The author is gone, but his manuscript is not. There are two copies of it. One is in the hands of a book editor by the name of Elvira Eveland. There's also the copy John sent to himself via registered mail that day you saw him at the post office. You see, there's a widespread belief among would-be authors that the way to prevent their work from being stolen by unscrupulous publishers is to send a copy to themselves registered mail as a means of proving not only their authorship, but the date by which it had been written. Some even go so far as to formally copyright their manuscripts, which is quite unnecessary because publishers do that for them. Therefore, if John did in fact mail a copy of the manuscript to himself, it must be somewhere in his house."

Kate slapped the table and lurched upright in her chair. "Oh gosh, Mrs. Bee, do you suppose that could have been the cause of Mr. Bohannon's murder?"

"I'm afraid you've lost me, my dear."

With a decisive nod, Murray said, "Me too."

"Suppose the person who killed Sara Griffith heard that Mr. Bohannon was writing a book about the case and decided he'd better get rid of Mr. Bohannon and the manuscript."

Beatrice slowly shook her head. "This is guesswork, my dear. We don't know what was in the book."

"We can easily find out. Mr. Bohannon sent a copy to himself. It must be somewhere in his house."

"Are you proposing we break into the house?"

"There's no need to break in," Kate said, smiling, "when you have a key to the door."

"We can't just go barging in," said Beatrice with eyes glinting mischievously. "We've got to have a plan."

25

As ELEANOR LEFT Beatrice's house through the front door, she declared as loudly as possible, "I hope your headache clears up soon, Bea. What you need is a long soak in a hot tub and then a nice nap. And take your phone off the hook."

Her purpose, according to the plan, was to foster among any curiosity seekers who might still be lingering on the street the impression that Beatrice was within the house while, in fact, she and Kate were going out the back door.

To Eleanor's disappointment and dismay, she discovered as she walked along Brookview Avenue that the street was quiet and unpopulated.

Arriving at her house, she supposed the absence of people was due to how cold it was outside and because with the body toted out and police cars gone, there was nothing left to see.

Now, if the plan were going properly, Eleanor thought as she closed her front door, Kate and Beatrice would have reached the alley beside Bohannon's one-story, red-brick house.

Indeed, at the very moment Eleanor closed her door, Beatrice whispered to Kate, "This is so thrilling." She peered around a corner of the front porch. "Not a soul in sight."

"Cross your fingers," said Kate, nervously, "that we're not spotted by some busybody looking out a window."

"No need to fret about that. The only busybody on this block is Eleanor, and fortunately for us, she's our ally."

"Be that as it may, I'm still nervous."

"The main thing, my dear, is not to *show* it."

Kate gulped the cold air.

"You must move boldly and confidently onto and across this porch," said Beatrice with a squeeze of Kate's shoulder. "Tell me when you're ready."

On a plume of steam, Kate answered, "It's now or never."

"Good show, my dear. Remember our plan. You wait here while I pretend to look into John's mailbox. If the coast is clear, I'll give you the high sign."

The signal was to be a tugging of the right earlobe. When it came, Kate was to make a dash from the alley, onto the porch, and across it. By the time she reached the door Beatrice would have it unlocked and standing open, allowing Kate to enter without a moment's pause. But as Beatrice lifted her right hand to execute the plan, a black

Packard touring sedan appeared as if out of nowhere to pass with excruciating slowness as the driver gazed at the house. But as the car slowed even more, the man at the wheel shouted at Beatrice, "Can you tell me how to get back on Bridge Street?"

With instructions given and earlobe tugged, Kate rushed to the door and in the house. Following her, Beatrice said, "Nicely done, my dear. I believe you've got all the instincts to become a truly superb criminal."

As as the door closed, Kate became conscious of the strong odor that had attracted Eleanor Murray's collie. With a shudder, she said, "The sooner we find what we've come here for and can get out of this house, the better I'll feel."

"I think the place to start searching is John's study," said Beatrice. "It used to be the dining room."

Evidence of the house owner's interests and profession were visible by the wall of bookcases jammed with volumes containing biographies of kings and queens, princes and pretenders, prime ministers and presidents, and both conquerors and rebels. Along with these books were bulky tomes recounting centuries of human struggles which John Bohannon had labored to teach to students in Robinsville High School for more than thirty years. Pausing in the doorway, Kate gazed at the other walls festooned with artifacts and memorabilia of the life of that man whose remains were now in the custody of Ed Polansky. Stepping into the room as she might enter a tomb, she said softly, "There's no question that a bachelor lived here. There's dust on everything."

"I once volunteered to come over weekly to tidy up the place for him," said Beatrice, unhesitatingly entering the room. "His reaction was exactly that of Sherlock Holmes when he discovered Mrs. Hudson had straightened up his rooms. You would have thought I somehow had threatened to disrupt the cosmic order."

"The place to begin looking, I suppose," said Kate, "is in the desk drawers."

"That would be typical of John," said Beatrice, "however, it's not where I'd choose to hide anything so valuable."

"Why should Mr. Bohannon believe his manuscript had value, other than as a backup copy in case the original was lost, or not returned by Elvira Eveland? I'm only guessing that's why he was murdered. Maybe he *was* just the victim of someone who chanced to break into this house."

"You're forgetting that Eleanor said the man she saw in her yard was going *in the direction of this house*. You take a look in the desk while I poke around behind some of those books." Striding purposefully toward the wall of bookcases, she said, blithely, "Since I was a young girl reading O. Henry's stories about Jimmy Valentine, and later E.W. Hornung's adventures of another cracksman, A. J. Raffles, I have felt enormous admiration for the daring and cunning of cat burglars and second-story men. They're so . . . gentlemanly."

"I doubt that you'd feel that way if you discovered one of them had purloined your jewelry."

"Any man who burglarized me would be sadly disappointed," Beatrice said as she pulled dusty books from shelves. "I do all my shopping at the Woolworth costume jewelry counter." A gasp from Kate turned her around expectantly. "What is it, my dear?"

Drawing a bulky package from the center drawer of the desk, Kate said exultantly, "I believe I may have found it."

"It's the right size for a manuscript," said Beatrice as she rushed to Kate.

"It's addressed to Mr. Bohannon," Kate said, holding up the package for Beatrice to see the mailing label. "And it was sent by registered mail. It's still sealed."

"Well, open it, my dear."

26

AYING THE LAST page of the manuscript atop the 185 others that formed the mystery novel, Kate muttered, "No, no, no."

A voice startled her. Turning toward the bedroom doorway, she found Paulie. "Whatcha reading?"

"Boy, you scared the daylights out of me."

"Sorry," he said, leaning against the jamb. "You missed a good *Grand Ole Opry* on the radio. Minnie Pearl was really funny." His attention turned to the pile of paper. "What's that?"

"It's a manuscript for a book. A murder mystery."

"Naturally. Is it a good one?"

"In some ways."

"I suppose you figured out who the murderer was before you got to the end, the way you usually do."

"In this instance I couldn't. The detective in the story

was confused. That's why he zeroed in on the wrong person."

"Is it one of those stories where the real killer framed somebody?"

"That's what happens in the book," Kate said. "Unfortunately, the author didn't realize that in the case on which he based his novel, the killer was even more clever than that. The real killer was able to arrange everything so neatly that the police who investigated the murder were unable to solve it."

"Are you going to explain all this to the person who wrote the book so he can fix it?"

"I'm afraid that's impossible," Kate said as she looked at her bedside clock and decided it was too late to telephone anyone. "He's dead. He was murdered because someone was afraid he would publish his book. The irony is that the book as it was written was a threat to no one."

For Beatrice Bradshaw, Sunday mornings differed from those of the rest of the week. First came a decision about whether to go to church. Although she believed in God and generally enjoyed the services offered by the Episcopal church, she felt no obligation to attend every week and stood ready to justify this stance to whoever dared to question her piety. The answer would be found in Mark, 2:27. In that Gospel verse Jesus rebuked similar critics of His approach to the Lord's day with, "The sabbath was made for man, and not man for the sabbath."

Deciding whether to attend church was more often than not a matter of looking out the window and judging the weather. Fair and warm usually meant yes. Wet or cold conditions, no. Anything between was a toss-up.

Should she feel the need to hear an uplifting sermon on a day with contrary weather, there were preachers on the radio.

Most significant about Sunday was not having to open the Book Nook. This afforded her the luxury of staying in bed an hour longer. She did not get a visit from Mary Edinger because Mary spent Sunday with a sister in Spring City, which meant not having to lay out breakfast for two. Instead of retrieving a copy of the *Independence* from the front porch, she brought in the much bulkier Philadelphia *Bulletin* with a section devoted to the reviews of new books and an enormous crossword puzzle.

This leisurely regimen also affected what she wore. During the week, her choice of clothes was dictated by the fact that she dealt with customers having the same notions of properly conservative dress as they would of the woman at the circulation desk when they went to the public library. On winter and fall days she wore a gray suit with a white or powder blue blouse. Spring and summer, she chose colorful long-sleeve dresses, alternating between flowered, patterned, and plain. But she never wore slacks, which she thought were just fine for slender young women like Kate Fallon, but inappropriate for anyone else. Weekday shoes were always sensible. Sundays, if she wished to, she could lounge around the house in floppy slippers, pajamas or nightgown, and bathrobe.

What she did not expect on this Sunday morning as she sat at the kitchen table eating toast with orange marmalade, chuckling at Dagwood Bumstead dashing out the door and slamming into the postman in her favorite comic strip *Blondie*, was the ring of the telephone. Flurried, she looked up from the paper. "Now who the dickens could that be?"

Having anticipated a wrong number, she was surprised to hear Kate Fallon, breathless with excitement. "Mrs. Bee, I have got to see you immediately."

At that moment, with deliciously slow pace, Scrappy MacFarland's Sunday was well under way. It had started with bringing in the Philadelphia *Bulletin* and *Inquirer* and sorting the sections in the order he intended to go through them. This routine always resulted in seven piles—comics, sports, rotogravure magazines, the week's radio listings and movie advertisements, national and international news sections, local news pages, and the editorials and columns. While consuming bacon and eggs, toast, orange juice, and coffee—the only day his breakfast was not prepared in the kitchen of the Vale-Rio Diner—he chuckled at Dagwood Bumstead bursting out the front door, slamming into the mailman, Mr. Beasley, and knocking him head over heels while the letters went flying. He then turned to *The Little King*, *Nancy*, *Felix the Cat*, *Li'l Abner*, and *Joe Palooka*. These were followed by the unfunny strips with continuing story lines: *Dick Tracy*, *Prince Valiant*, *Mandrake the Magician*, and *Little Orphan Annie*.

Finished eating and settled into an enormous armchair in the living room, he read columns by Louis Sobol (Broadway), Dorothy Kilgallen and Walter Winchell (gossip), and Walter Lippmann and Westbrook Pegler (news analysis and commentary).

An interruption in this routine, such as the telephone ringing, was decidedly unwelcome. Consequently, when he picked up the phone to hear Beatrice Bradshaw's voice, he answered gruffly, "MacFarland here. What is it?"

"Sorry to disturb your Sunday, Mr. MacFarland," she said, "but I wonder if I might impose on you for a few minutes of your precious time this morning? I assure you it's matter of utmost importance, else I wouldn't have bothered you on your day off."

"In the newspaper game," he said with a chuckle, "there's no such thing as a day off. Where and when?"

"Is it convenient to come to my home now? I've made a batch of scones you enjoy so much. And Kate Fallon is here now."

"Kate? What's she got to do with this?"

"She'll explain everything. Can you come now?"

Gazing disappointedly at the unread papers, he sighed. "May I take time to shave and get into some proper clothes?"

"Dress warmly, my dear. It's quite chilly this morning."

— Part 5 —

Who Killed
Nancy Edinger?

27

"So, Beatrice," said Scrappy MacFarland, sniffing the delicious aroma of freshly baked scones as she helped him take off his overcoat, "what's so important that you've gotten me out of bed at this ungodly hour?"

"Kate Fallon will explain. She's in the kitchen.

He found her looking pert and pretty and seated at the table with her right hand atop a thick block of typing paper. "May I assume, Kate," he said, "that whatever you are guarding is connected with my being here?"

"You may. It's a copy of the manuscript of a book written by John Bohannon. It's based on the murder of Sara Griffith."

"So that's why Bohannon was rooting around in the *Independence* archives," Scrappy said as he plopped into a chair. "That's the beauty of writing fiction. By changing the names of the real people you're free to twist facts to suit your plot. Did you find it a good read?"

"I'm sorry to say that as a mystery writer Mr. Bohannon was not very good. He had all the clues, but the detective in his story failed to see where they pointed. Just as the police today are wrong in suspecting Freddy Johnson of murdering Nancy Edinger, Mr. Bohannon's sleuth whom he has named Jake Elwell, suspected the wrong person in the murder of the elderly woman in the story. Both Mr. Bohannon and his alter ego in the form of Jake Elwell missed the true culprit."

"This is all very interesting," said Scrappy as he helped himself to a scone, "but so what?"

"So what? The man who killed Sara Griffith not only has been able to get away with it, but I believe he's added others to his list of victims. I refer, of course, to Nancy Edinger, Jonas Lonacre, and now Mr. Bohannon. I'm not clear as to the motive in the first two, but in Mr. Bohannon's case it has to have been the killer's fear of being exposed as the murderer of Sara Griffith. The killer knew Mr. Bohannon was writing a book and went to his house to find it and to eliminate him. He did just that on the Monday night after the V-for Victory Rally."

Slowly lathering a scone with honey, Scrappy smiled patiently. "How do you know that?"

"Mr. Bohannon was last seen on Saturday. Then you must consider Mrs. Murray's dog."

"Mrs. Murray's dog?"

"Its barking on Monday night prompted Mrs. Murray to report a prowler."

"But none was found."

"By the time the police came, he'd gone. But not before leaving the note."

"What note?"

Beatrice answered, "The morning after John was murdered, the milkman, Mr. Groover, found a note from John stating that he'd gone away on a fishing trip."

"As long as I've known Bohannon he's been going on fishing trips."

"Yes, that's a fact," said Kate, "but he never went away without telling Mrs. Bee."

Beatrice nodded emphatically. "True."

"In addition to not informing Mrs. Bee," Kate continued, "Mr. Bohannon did not tell anyone else he'd be away. He didn't suspend deliveries of the *Independence*. Nor did he inform the mailman, Mr. Granick."

"Newspapers and mail don't go sour if they're left on a porch a few days."

"Joke all you care to," Kate said impatiently. "However, I believe that note was left by the man Eleanor Murray told police she'd seen sneaking through her backyard. But he wasn't simply a prowler. He was going to Bohannon's house to stop the work on his book and to destroy whatever he'd written."

"Hold it right there. How did this person know, number one, that such a manuscript existed, and two, that it was a book about the Griffith murder?"

Beatrice answered, "John made no secret of the fact that he was writing one based on the Griffith case."

"Ah, there's the flaw in your plot, ladies. If Bohannon knew who'd really murdered that old woman, why on earth would he come out and tell the killer he was writing a book?"

"That's my point. Because he'd come to the wrong conclusion, he *didn't* know he was actually talking about his book *with* the *real* killer. It proved a fatal mistake."

Scrappy lifted the abandoned honey-coated scone and studied it as if were a priceless gemstone. "Assuming for the moment that what you say is accurate and based on your reading of Bohannon's book, have you concluded who really killed Sara Griffith?"

"Yes.

"Ah, this is the moment in mystery yarns," Scrappy said with a chuckle as he chomped into the scone, "where the plot takes the dramatic twist." Like the darting tongue of a bullfrog catching a fly, Scrappy's tongue snatched a droplet of honey drizzling from the scone. "This theory of yours assumes that the man who killed Sara Griffith knew that Bohannon had written, or was writing, a book about it. Would you have me believe that Bohannon, knowing who killed the old lady, went ahead and told the killer about the book?"

"Mr. Bohannon made no secret of what he was working on. But as I told you, he'd made a mistake. He placed blame for the murder on the wrong man."

"And now you think you know the name of that man?"

"I do. But I have no proof. That's where you come in."

"Ah-ha, now the plot really thickens!"

"I want you to run a story in the *Independence* to the effect that I have the manuscript."

Reddening with anger from neck to forehead, Scrappy shook his head. "No way!"

Kate shrugged. "Very well, you leave me no choice but to spread the story myself. You know very well how the people of Robinsville love to spread gossip. Between Mrs. Bee and me, the whole town will be buzzing."

Scrappy glowered. "This is blackmail."

28

PRECISELY AT FIVE o'clock Monday morning to the satisfying rumble of the press in the basement, Scrappy MacFarland clipped an Upmann double corona cigar made in Cuba and winked across his desk at Dick Levitan, declaring, "As somebody once said, 'The game is afoot.'"

Levitan's eyes turned down to a proof of the front page of the newspaper and read the banner headline:

MANUSCRIPT MAY HOLD KEY TO GRIFFITH MURDER

The story Scrappy had spent the night writing began, "A copy of the manuscript of a book written by murder victim John Bohannon, retired Robinsville High School history teacher, may contain evidence which could lead to the killer of Sara Griffith, according to Miss Kate Fallon, the young woman who found the manuscript in the Bohannon house."

With a scowl, Levitan said, "Scrappy, I can't believe you're going along with this Fallon girl's harebrained idea."

"There's method in the madness," said Scrappy, puffing a plume of smoke as he picked up the receiver of a black-candlestick telephone and dialed. With a smile at Levitan, he said into the phone, "By ten o'clock this morning the *Independence* will be landing on doorsteps and going into mailboxes all over town. I trust you're ready.

The voice on the phone replied, "In case you haven't noticed, it's been snowing hard since midnight. The weather bureau says we'll get five or six inches by noon."

"I assure you, a little snow has yet to keep this newspaper from getting out."

"There's always a first time for everything. Maybe we should call this thing off."

"I'm afraid it's too late for that."

"What if he doesn't go for it?"

"He has to, so this is no time for you to go wobbly."

"Where will you be?"

"Right here waiting for your call."

Even without looking through the window of her bedroom, Kate Fallon had become aware that the spattering of the thick snowflakes on the pane meant it was the kind which would accumulate quickly, kindling hope in children of Paulie's age that schools would be closed for the day, perhaps even two days. It had started falling a little after midnight, and if her memory of such days when she had been a schoolgirl were good measure, she expected that by the time she got out of bed at six o'clock the bare trees and brown lawns of Pennsylvania Avenue would have a sort of cotton-candy look. For a little while the whole town would be wrapped in a wonderful silence lasting only as long as it took for men and boys to get shovels from garages and cellars in order to unleash a discordant symphony of metal scraping on pavements.

Lying in bed and enjoying the aroma of coffee brewing in the kitchen, she found herself thinking of Mike and wondering if snow were also falling on his camp down in South Carolina. Closing her eyes, she remembered Mike before the war, picturing him on such a morning, brushing snow off his car, digging it out and laboring to put chains on the back tires, only to have a town snowplow come along the street to shove the snow aside and trap the car worse than before.

Presently, she heard a muffled chuck-chuck-chuck of a set of tire chains coming up Pennsylvania Avenue from the direction of the West End firehouse and then stopping with its motor running in front of the house. With her heart suddenly gripped in an icy hand she heard the clinking and rattling of milk bottles in Mr. Groover's metal basket. Breathless and with hands trembling, she left the bed and moved to the window. Parting fleecy curtains and peering down, she was surprised to see hurrying back to the truck not Mr. Groover, but his son Johnny.

A moment later, her mother called from below. "Kate, are you up? Get a move on, hon. Your breakfast will be ready in a couple of minutes."

When Kate entered the warm kitchen a few minutes

later Mrs. Fallon said, "It's been snowing hard all night. I think maybe you should take a leaf from Mr. Groover's book and not go to work today. He sent his boy out on the route instead."

"I have to go to work," Kate said firmly as her mother carried a plate of bacon and eggs to the table. "The war effort's not going to stop on account of a little snow."

29

NOT SURPRISINGLY, THE Bridge Street bus was over-due. But as Kate turned her back to a biting wind and resigned herself to being late for work, a black-and-white Ford sedan belonging to the Robinsville Police Force emerged from the driving snow and stopped beside her. Rolling down a window, Jim Kerner said, "Hello, Kate. What are you doing out in this weather?"

"Obviously, I'm waiting for the bus to take me to my job."

"I heard you've taken up welding."

"That's right."

"Well, I'm afraid you're going to be late getting to work this morning. I've got orders to bring you to head-quarters."

"Orders? From whom?"

"Who else? Detwiler wants to talk to you about the item about you in today's paper."

"Well, you can tell your boss he'll have to wait to talk to me after work."

"There's no use in arguing, Kate. The chief is worried about your safety. As am I. So, you can forget about work for the moment and get in the car."

"Am I under arrest?"

"No, but if you don't get in the car, you will be."

"Oh, very well," she said as he reached across the front seat to open a door, "but this is really a waste of time. Yours, his, and mine."

As she settled into the seat, he asked, "Is that newspaper article true?"

"I can't say. I haven't read it."

"It says you've got a copy of Bohannon's manuscript and that you've got an idea as to who killed Sara Griffith. Is that right?"

"Yes it is."

"You should have come to me about it, Kate," said Kerner as the car pulled away from the curb. "After all, I was in charge of that investigation. If you'd come to me, I could have kept you from getting yourself in serious trouble. Did it not occur to you that by talking to Scrappy MacFarland about that manuscript you were putting yourself on the spot?"

"Of course it occurred to me. That was the objective. I wanted to force the hand of the man who murdered Sara Griffith. The irony is that killing Mr. Bohannon was unnecessary because the book he wrote based on the Griffith murder would not have posed a threat to Sara's killer."

"Is that so? Why not?"

Kate gazed at snow streaming toward the windshield. "There are two reasons. First, in the book Mr. Bohannon's detective came up with the wrong suspect. He pinned the killing on a young man who was very loosely inspired by Jonas Longacre. His reasoning in suspecting the Jonas Longacre character was very flimsy at best. But as subsequent events have shown, the person who killed Mr. Bohannon in an effort to keep the book from being published could not have been Jonas Longacre. Jonas was found dead in the ruins of the Gordon factory *before* Mr. Bohannon was killed."

"And the second reason?"

"Mr. Bohannon's book is the worst detective novel I've ever read. I simply can't imagine any publisher taking it on. Of course, the killer couldn't know that, could he? He might not have realized it even if he'd succeeded in finding the manuscript and taken time to read it."

"Where did you find the manuscript?"

"It was in a desk drawer in a large envelope addressed to Mr. Bohannon. He'd sent it to himself by registered mail as a means of certifying his copyright. Obviously the killer had never heard of that practice of novice authors."

"So the manuscript was in that house all the time," Kerner said as the police car picked up speed on the snow-clogged street. "That's pretty funny."

"Excuse me, Jim," said Kate, lightly touching his shoulder, "but don't you think you're going too fast for the conditions? I would like to get to the station in one piece."

"You're not going to the station, Kate."

Kate's eyes went wide. "I beg your pardon?"

"I'm sorry, Kate," said Kerner gravely as his right hand moved from the steering wheel to his holstered pistol. "I just can't let you go any further with this."

With snow pellets pinging against the windshield and an icy awakening of horror knotting in her chest, Kate gasped, "Oh my gosh, Jim. It was . . . you?"

He let out a bark of a laugh. "I thought you knew."

"No, but I can see it now."

"Understanding is always easier after you've gotten a confession."

"Yes, it's becoming quite clear. As the chief investigator of the Griffith murder you were able to ensure that it wouldn't be solved."

"I know you're a great reader of detective stories, Kate, but you're way off base on this one. No, I did not kill Sara Griffith. But I very quickly discovered who did. And I'm sorry to say that you are also wrong in dismissing the man whom you say was suspected by the detective in Bohannon's book. I have no idea what name Bohannon gave the killer he patterned on Jonas Longacre, or why Bohannon concluded that character was the murderer, but in fact the old lady *was* killed by Jonas Longacre. It wasn't intentional, however. Jonas and his gang were in Sara's house to pull a burglary. They thought the old lady was not at home. But she caught them in the act and very bravely, but foolishly, tried to stop them. Jonas gave her a shove, she hit her head on a corner of a table as she fell, and that was that. I suppose it was inevitable that as that trio went around pulling burglaries they'd make a mistake. In that instance they did. They killed the old lady. And for the first time they left a clue that led me right to Jonas. Somehow, the poor sap's wallet fell out of his pocket."

"You knew Jonas had been there when Sara was killed," said Kate incredulously, "yet you didn't question him?"

"Sure I questioned him. And I got a confession, not only to Griffith's killing, but to a series of burglaries."

"Why you didn't arrest him and the others?"

"I guess you could say it was out of spite."

"Out of *spite*? For whom?

"Because you're a woman, you probably won't understand."

"Try me."

"Okay, here it is. Two days before the Griffith murder I decided to enlist in the Marines. But after I had the physical examination they told me I'd failed. I was classified 4-F. I couldn't believe it! I was deemed unfit to go out and fight Japs, but there was nothing to keep me from continuing to work as a cop. The whole episode left me bitter. Where's the glory in being a cop when there is a war to be fought? Compared to going to war for my country, what's capturing a gang of teenage burglars to me? Well, Jonas Longacre gave me the answer. If I were to let him and his two pals Perillo and Flynn go, they'd cut me in on the substantial proceeds of the Griffith burglary and all the other jobs they planned to pull. Unfortunately, their plans left a great deal to be desired. That's when I decided I had to take over. I couldn't risk them getting caught and spilling the beans about the Griffith murder and implicating me. It was easy. I simply made sure they wouldn't get caught. That's why all the recent burglaries happened when I was on overnight patrol duty. I found a lot of satisfaction in having come up with a way to compensate myself for being forced to work those hours because of a shortage of manpower caused by so many guys going off to a war I'd been declared unfit to fight."

"Why did it suddenly became necessary to kill Jonas?"

"The jerk was rapidly developing a drinking problem. When he got stewed, he became a blabbermouth. Unfortunately, he babbled to a wise guy who decided to cut himself in on the action. Well, I couldn't allow that, could I? Care to venture a guess as to that guy's name?"

Kate slowly shook her head.

"No? I'm disappointed, Kate. But this is real life, not one of your mystery novels, right?"

"Unhappily."

"The guy Jonas blabbed to was none other than the man I intend to arrest for the murder of your friend Nancy Edinger."

"Freddy Johnson!"

"Of course. His being dumped by Nancy made him the perfect fall guy."

Kate chuckled, "My little brother was right. A frame-up."

"Freddy will certainly do his best to wiggle out of it by telling what he knows about the burglary ring and my connection to it. But no one is going to believe anything that comes from the mouth of the murderer of such a pretty and popular girl. The case I'm putting together will land Freddy on death row. Ironically, the jerk will have brought it on himself by having a very a public argument with Nancy outside the Vale-Rio Diner, an argument witnessed by the milkman. But not only by Mr. Groover. I was there, too. I'd just finished my overnight tour and was having my breakfast. I looked out the window and saw immediately how to handle the Freddy problem. I had been worried that Freddy spilled the beans to Nancy. Here was a way to kill two birds with one stone . . . so to speak. On that morning, just as I've done with you today, I took Nancy for a ride in a police car."

"But just as you figured you'd gotten away with all this," said Kate, "you discovered that Mr. Bohannon was writing a book based on the Griffith murder."

"I didn't *discover* it. He told me about it. He even asked for my help and advice. I hoped to handle the problem of his damned book by staging a burglary. Two things went wrong."

"He surprised you, as Sara had surprised Jonas."

"Yes, except that there was nothing accidental about Bohannon's demise."

"The second thing that went wrong was that you couldn't find the manuscript."

"I might have if I'd had time to search further. But that busybody Murray woman called the police. I beat a hasty exit out the back door as Doebling and Ludlum were pulling up in front of the house. If they'd conducted an investigation, they would have found Bohannon's body. Later, I read their report and saw who had made the complaint about a prowler. Under the circumstances, I probably would have handled it the way they did. In any event, I certainly was not in a position to criticize their actions."

"If you left the house while the police were out in front, how and when did you leave the note for the milkman? That was a clever touch."

"Thank you. It came as an afterthought. I went back to the house two hours later. I wanted to buy time so that I could resume looking for the manuscript. However, on reflection, I realized that with the author dead, I had nothing to fear from him or whatever he'd written in his book. Until I picked up this morning's paper and read about you. I'm sorry about this, Kate. I always liked you. In the tenth grade I was in love with you. Then you fell for Mike King. He's in for a rough time, once your body is found."

"You'll never get away with it, Jim. Detwiler will wonder why you didn't bring me in."

"Again you disappoint me, Kate. Detwiler knows nothing about this."

"Someone will have seen you pick me up at the bus stop."

"Unlikely in this snowstorm. But if someone did see, I'll admit it. I picked you up because I'd read the story in the paper and was concerned for your safety. I let you off at your new job and never saw you again. Who's going to doubt me? People always believe a cop."

Two hours later, sitting in a Vale-Rio Diner booth with Scrappy MacFarland and Chief Detwiler, Kate thought about how the end of the drama in Jim Kerner's police car had seemed to unfold like a Saturday matinee movie at the Rialto with Paulie beside her, wide-eyed on the edge of his seat and shoving Jujubes candies into his mouth—the sudden blare of sirens, lights of another police car flashing on and off as it overtook Kerner's, windows of the second car being rolled down, a thrusting hand with a pistol in it, and Chief Detwiler bellowing melodramatically, "Pull over, Jim. The jig is up."

"I thought I was a dead woman," she said as a waitress placed heaping plates of scrapple before MacFarland and bacon and eggs in front of Detwiler. "Suddenly, there you two were like the cavalry. How did you manage to do it?"

Detwiler smiled proudly. "Scrappy and I were following you from the second you left our house."

"I saw no one following me."

"Young lady," said the police chief, "that's exactly what you should expect when I follow you."

"You must have been surprised by Kerner showing up at the bus stop."

"No. When Scrappy telephoned me and related the plan I was positive Kerner would see that he had no choice but to make his move."

"Are you telling me that you already knew he'd killed Mr. Bohannon?"

"That conclusion was forced upon me later. What I suspected him of from the beginning was that he was setting up the Johnson boy to take the fall for killing the Edinger girl. Jim is a good cop, but he was just too quick off the mark in zeroing in on Johnson. I asked myself why he was in such a rush to judge. Then came the Jonas Longacre murder, and suddenly Jim was trying to pin that on Johnson and getting very upset with me for not letting him arrest the kid. I saw a possible link between Johnson and Longacre and that perhaps it involved the Edinger girl. You know, a boy-girl-boy thing. Your proverbial lovers' triangle. But then came the Bohannon murder. While there was the possibility of a link between the first two cases in the person of Freddy Johnson, with jealousy a possible motive, I couldn't imagine why he'd kill Bohannon. And that's where I found myself when Scrappy phoned to tell me about Bohannon's book, along with your idea, Kate, to try to force the hand of the killer. Who in his wildest dream could have seen that your bold but extremely perilous plan was to result in solving *four* homicides. And the breaking up of a burglary ring. Perillo and Flynn are being arrested by Doebling and Ludlum even as we speak."

"And all of this happened, Kate," interjected Scrappy, "because your expertise in the field of mystery novels led you to detect the flaw of reasoning in Bohannon's manuscript. What interests me now is knowing which of the characters in Bohannon's book you thought should have been revealed as the killer."

"Oh, it should have been the editor of the town newspaper. No doubt about it."

About the Author

When the Japanese attacked United States navy and army bases at Pearl Harbor, Hawaii, on Sunday, December 7, 1941, M. T. Jefferson was seven years old, the youngest of five children in a family very much like the Fallons, and residing in a small Pennsylvania steel town. Jefferson grew up to be a journalist and author of more than forty books and now lives in New York City.

PENGUIN PUTNAM INC.
Online

Your Internet gateway to a virtual environment with
hundreds of entertaining and enlightening books
from Penguin Putnam Inc.

*While you're there, get the latest buzz on
the best authors and books around—*

Tom Clancy, Patricia Cornwell, W.E.B. Griffin,
Nora Roberts, William Gibson, Robin Cook,
Brian Jacques, Catherine Coulter, Stephen King,
Jacquelyn Mitchard, and many more!

**Penguin Putnam Online is located at
http://www.penguinputnam.com**

PENGUIN PUTNAM NEWS

Every month you'll get an inside look at our upcoming
books and new features on our site. This is an
ongoing effort to provide you with the most
up-to-date information about
our books and authors.

**Subscribe to Penguin Putnam News at
http://www.penguinputnam.com/ClubPPI**